Examining life up close, selecting characters from it, portraying them from various perspectives enhances the authenticity of the writer's creations. He doesn't claim to have experienced 'real-life as it is' anywhere. Nor does he engage in parallel movements. Despite being a journalist, he preserves the art of storytelling from his own life. He is deeply influenced by idealistic authors like Tolstoy and Jainendra Kumar. He has read Kaka Saheb Kalelkar and Vishnu Sakharam Khandekar.

Dr. Prabhakar Machwe
RENOWNED WRITER AND LINGUIST

Dark Water is a tragedy, 'the tragedy of humanity, because within a person, there is Dark Water— the ocean of life values.' The author has not only seen the characters of this 'Dark Water' up close but has also heard their heartbeats. That's why each character is alive and meaningful. That's why the tragedy could be so profound and impactful.

Vishnu Prabhakar
PROMINENT WRITER, SAHITYA AKADEMI AWARD WINNER

Himanshu Joshi has set many milestones in his narrative journey. Perhaps the diversity found in his works is unmatched by his contemporaries in the art of storytelling. The primary reason for this might be that he has witnessed numerous ups and downs in his challenging life, and this reflection is evident in his writings.

Kusum Kumar
WELL-KNOWN WRITER, SANGEET NATAK AKADEMI AWARD WINNER

DARK WATER

A Novel

Himanshu Joshi

ISBN: 978-93-56825-96-3
eISBN: 978-93-56829-34-3

Prabhakar Prakashan (P) Ltd.
Plot No.-55, Main Mother Dairy Road
Pandav Nagar, East Delhi-110092
Phone: 011-40395855
WhatsApp: +91 9319228272
E-mail: sales@pharosbooks.in
Website: www.prabhakarprakashan.com
First Edition: 2023

Printed By: Sushma Book Binding House, Okhla
Industrial Area, Phase II, New Delhi-110020

DARK WATER
By Himanshu Joshi

PUBLISHER'S NOTE

In the vast realm of literature, there exists a work that transcends the ordinary, a narrative that immerses itself fully into the very essence of existence. "Dark Water," as we shall come to know it, is a story where the ceaseless ebb and flow of ocean waves mirror the intricate dance of human lives. Just as the sea stands resolute against nature's whims, this literary masterpiece is an unwavering and poignant tale. At times, it roars with the tempestuous intensity of a squall at sea, while at others, it whispers with the gentle caress of waves upon a tranquil shore. It is a profound odyssey, an exploration of the unfathomable richness concealed within its pages.

The author, Himanshu Joshi, is a luminary in both literature and journalism. With a masterful blend of fact and fiction, Joshi embarks on a literary journey that transcends the ordinary. His storytelling is rooted in the traditions of realism, yet intricately weaves each character and experience into the very fabric of life itself. As readers delve into "Dark Water," they will unearth a story where Joshi artfully intertwines his own life with the intricate destinies of his characters, creating a literary work that resonates with universal truths.

Originally published in 1971, "Dark Water" dared to venture into uncharted literary waters, casting its discerning eye upon the enigmatic Andaman and Nicobar Islands. Set against the vibrant backdrop of Kolkata, a city adorned with idiosyncrasies and unmistakable identity, the narrative embarks on a journey that traverses not only geographical landscapes but also the profound emotional terrain of its characters. This expedition, marked by moments of eager anticipation and tranquil introspection, ultimately leads to the captivating atmosphere of the Andaman and Nicobar Islands.

Within these remote islands, Joshi masterfully paints a world steeped in authenticity—a world where life is shaped by the absence of luxuries, the relentless exploitation of labour, and the enduring grip of age-old superstitions. Amidst this challenging milieu, the character of Saket emerges as a guiding light for transformative change. He aligns himself with the oppressed, and his unwavering enthusiasm becomes a catalyst for profound shifts in the social fabric. The narrative broadens its scope, transcending individual experiences to explore the broader societal context, particularly in relationships such as that between Neena and Saket, and the evolving dynamics between Saket and Deep Di.

Renowned author Vishnu Prabhakar, an esteemed literary figure celebrated for his profound insights, extensive body of work, and winner of prestigious awards, offers his profound commentary on "Dark Water":

> "This story of unfulfilled love, shaped by the heart-wrenching transformation of Saket, resonates deeply. The character of Saket, who slowly but surely progresses, is the central figure in this narrative. He becomes a symbol of resilience and the will to live. The tragic ending of the story reflects the immense tragedy that has become a part of our lives today, where we are forced to do things that are detrimental to us. The author has brilliantly captured the essence of the Nicobar Islands with simple, straightforward language and vivid symbolism."

Vrajendra Gaur, another esteemed author, a recipient of the Filmfare Award and renowned film scriptwriter and dialogue writer, reflects on the narrative style and expansiveness:

> "The vast expanse of 'Dark Water' is truly reflective of its name. Just as the characters within it possess vast and profound hearts, the narrative style mirrors the powerful, boundless ocean, where characters collide like waves with the towering rocks in the midst of the ocean."

As publisher, we take immense delight in presenting this remarkable literary work to you. "Dark Water," a translation of Himanshu Joshi's creation "Mahasagar", is a masterpiece that invites you to embark on a transformative journey through its pages.

Moreover, this narrative holds the distinction of being the first novel in Hindi literature to delve into the captivating landscapes of the Andaman and Nicobar Islands, further enriching its significance. With these profound words from renowned authors Vishnu Prabhakar and Vrajendra Gaur, we invite you to immerse yourself in the depths of "Dark Water," where tragedy and transformation converge in a timeless exploration of the human condition. We are delighted to share this remarkable book with you, confident that it will leave an indelible mark on your literary voyage, forever etching its name, "Dark Water," into your memory.

PRABHAKAR PRAKASHAN
DELHI, INDIA

DEDICATED

To those characters of this novel who had scattered all around me while my stay in Andaman and Nicobar Islands

—Himanshu Joshi

TWO WORDS

I witnessed a few events up close, examined some individuals closely. Saket, Deep, Chhaya, Neena—these characters were all around me in one way or another. I have endeavored to bring them together here.

What is as close as life is just as natural—this has always been my belief from the beginning. So, as much as possible, I have refrained from showcasing any "magic."

It's not just me who saw Dada Babu pushing his cart; many others have witnessed it too. I still remember the day when the municipal truck took away his cart, and he wandered around like a madman from house to house all day long. Deep's school was not far from my house. Saket remained my constant friend for years. The eucalyptus tree still stands there just as before. Yes, some things have aged. The house where Saket used to live now houses someone else. When I pass by there, it seems as if moments from cinema are unfolding right before my eyes. While writing all this, I can't help but wonder if, alongside all these characters, I am also a character! Perhaps, knowingly or unknowingly, I am not writing about myself! It's possible that as you read, you might also see a reflection of yourself somewhere! If that happens, then I would consider my effort successful.

Himanshu Joshi
7/C-2, Hindustan Times Apartments
Mayur Vihar, Phase-One, Delhi-110091

DARK WATER

ONE

He was still in a dilemma when the door gently opened.

Roop entered, and after leaving a cup of tea, went back. Saket looked at Roop and then at the cup.

Roop needed a saree. She had been managing with a single saree for some time past. Anni had asked for some money yesterday to go on a picnic. He had said that all the boys in his class were going, but how could he go without shoes; Chhaya rarely moved out of the house. She had weak eyes since her childhood. But now she was not able to see even what she could see as a child. Confining herself within the four walls of the house, she covered herself with Roop's clothes.

He intended to look for a couple of tuitions after his examinations were over. Or, he would try to find a part-time job. But the examinations had not even started. When would they get over-when? He was in a fix.

He drew the cup towards himself. He kept staring at two thin transparent streaks of steam rising above the cup.

Sip... Sip.... he took the cup to his lips a couple of times and kept it back. There was a wet round mark on the bottom of the cup where he had kept it before.

He stretched his limbs and got up after some thought. He opened the window half. An oblique beam of sunshine penetrating through the glass screen of the window formed a pattern on the floor. The dust in the room looked bright. It looked as though all the things were bereft of their covering and stood out in their naked, original form.

He shifted the chair a little forward so that the whole yellow patch of sunlight would completely envelop him.

He sat on the chair, resting comfortably against its back. He stretched his legs to their full length and fixed his gaze on the ceiling as though he was searching for something.

Suddenly his eyes came to rest on a hazy photograph hung on the wall in front of him, and remained stuck there. Khadi dress. An overgrowth of beard. Hands linked together. Heavy shackles on his feet. A garland of withered flowers around the frame had acquired a dull appearance because of dust and smoke.

It was the photograph of his deceased father. He wondered who had brought that photograph there and how. Till his mother was alive, that photograph used to be kept along with her Gods. Every year on August 15, the mother used to put a garland of fresh flowers on that photograph. On the same day, his mother used to perform his father's shraddha ceremony. The garland which now hung on the photograph was the one put there on the last August 15 in his mother's life… Perhaps she…perhaps…

"Bhaiya, is it a holiday for you today?"

Saket got up in confusion when Roop woke him up from his reverie. He closed the half-open book which had fallen on his lap and put it on the table. He gulped down the remaining tea which had gone cold.

He had a quick wash and started dressing up. He wore his usual closed coat of woollen Khadi. He put on his chappals. He combed his hair without looking into the mirror and tucked a couple of books under his arm. As he started going down the stairs whistling, he heard wailing and quarrelling in the house.

He stopped while he was about to put his foot on the last step.

"Roop!"

Roop was cleaning the utensils that had been used the previous night. Hearing Saket's voice, she came hurrying. Keeping her dark hands away from her body, she stood there hesitating.

"Who is crying inside?"

"Must be Anni, Bhaiya".

"Why? What has happened?"

"Nothing," She merely shook her head.

"You must have beaten him," Saket said with sweet admonition.

Before Roop would give any reply, Chhaya, who was leaning against the wall, blurted out: "Ammi has beaten him, Dadda."

"Why?"

"He was asking for roti."

"Then give him roti. Why should he cry for it?"

No one gave any reply to him. Saket was almost in a panic when all of them looked at him in silence.

His hand came to rest on his chin. A small frown appeared on his forehead. Moistening his lips with the tip of his tongue he said: "Is the ration in the house exhausted?"

Even now Roop remained silent. She uttered not a word.

Saket's feet remained fixed like steel to the spot where he stood. He had been managing his night meals somewhere outside. When he had returned home late last night, everybody had been asleep. The fire in the hearth had been put out. There had been the same hue and cry, last night as well with Chhoti Ma beating her children mercilessly.

The pressure on his lower lip from the two rows of teeth was so great, it left two or three deep marks on the flesh.

"Why didn't you tell me yesterday?" Saket demanded in such a tone that Roop panicked. "Haven't I told you that when you're about to run out of anything, you must inform me a day or two in advance?"

"I did tell you," Roop said in a frightened tone. "But you were reading and perhaps it didn't register."

"Yes, you had told me?" Saket said to himself as it were.

He was wondering what had gone wrong with him. He had been forgetting everything lately... Last evening, he had looked for his pen all over the house but the pen was tucked in the pocket! The day before yesterday, there was Mamaji's letter saying that he had forgotten to affix the stamp to the envelope... And his cousin Prabodh had asked in his letter what the point was in fixing stamps worth sixty paise on the same envelope.

The shade of the tree had spread like water spilt on a floor. The empty road gave the impression of being very wide. In the corporation park, there were flashes of yellow flowers here and there. And the dark green colour of the leaves in the sun...

Despite having walked for long, Saket felt as though he was in the same spot where he had started. He couldn't decide which direction he should take.

Rattan wouldn't have returned from Bilaspur yet. Tai, his mother must be still at the hospital. The house must be locked...

The palm tree in front had grown really very tall today.

He had no courage to go to the grocer's shop. He hadn't yet been able to pay the arrears. Neither was he certain as to when he would be able to do it.

It was Sunday, a holiday. He was sure Deep Di would be at home. Deep Di was the very embodiment of a home. Thick Khadi curtains with a large floral print, windows half open to the blue sky, shutters, walls, ceiling, floor of ebony and nothing but doors all around.

There was a scooter parked outside. Deep Di had been telling him that Sisir Babu was very keen on getting her a transfer. Sisir Babu was an animal — a carnivorous animal. Although he dressed in khadi clothes, he was capable of devouring human flesh.

Saket could not take a step forward. At every step, his foot rose with great difficulty only to get stuck on the same spot. He stopped midway on the stairs for a few moments and then hurriedly walked down with noisy steps.

Winter time — did it take long before it is seven in the evening?

He was late just half an hour, he thought. He might as well go for his tuition. His pupil was having her terminal examinations the following day.

Without much thought his steps turned towards a narrow lane where a whole lot of crows remained perched on the neem tree, where the windows on both sides of the road were always open, where a woman was seen looking out of every window.

Respectable people do not pass along that street. But Saket had to pass through that very notorious lane. But Saket cast his gaze nowhere — he found those centuries-old animate Khajuraho pictures meaningless.

He disappeared into a big house in another lane.

TWO

"You're again late today, Sir!"

Saket didn't like to be addressed in such terms. He didn't react to that comment. He gently drew his chair and sank into it as usual.

The girls' eyes were fixed on an already opened book.

"What have you been reading?"

"Nothing, Sir!" she looked up very innocently. "It's a book."

"I too can see that it's a book. But what book?"

"Nothing particular, Sir," she laughed. I'm reading the railway timetable. Sir!" she said in a halting tone.

Saket was angry and amused at the same time.

"What is the paper you have to write tomorrow?" He made a face and asked in the same tone.

"Elementary Hindi."

"What has Elementary Hindi to do with the railway timetable?"

" It has, Sir!" she said innocently. "I've to write an essay on travel and I'm trying to find out the train timings, Sir!"

"Do you know meters and figures of speech?"

"Nn…o…!"

"Well then, take out your book."

She casually picked up a book from a pile. Saket who was in a dejected mood, started teaching her. He knew that this girl didn't want to pass the examination under any circumstances, still, he didn't want to leave anything undone.

The tuition was over and he was ready to leave.

"Do you have anything more to ask?"

"I want to know one thing, Sir!"

"Not one or two.... ask me ten things!"

"Devdas about whom a film has also been made, was Gandhiji's son, wasn't he?"

"No, he was somebody else."

"They say in our class..." she said looking at him with great curiosity. "They say that Maithili Saranji wrote his book Saket on you. Isn't that right, Sir?"

He couldn't help laughing. He burst into a guffaw. He wondered when that girl, who was stupid like a camel, would have any sense.

That stupid girl perhaps felt abashed. Perhaps she had asked the wrong question. To get over that feeling, she asked another question:" Sir, Katty says that the story of Devdas is true — it must be true, isn't it, Sir?"

"Yes, yes, true — one hundred and one per cent true!"

The girl was naturally happy that what she had said turned out to be correct. And she asked with greater curiosity, "Sir, have you seen Devdas? You too used to live in Calcutta, isn't it?" Saket grew somewhat serious. He somehow swallowed his anger and nodded: "Yes."

"Where did you see him, Sir — in Calcutta?"

"Yes."

"In that case, you must have really known him personally!"

Saket shut the book and stood up. Hunger and questions of this nature made him lose his cool. He gesticulated with his hands somewhat dramatically: "Yes, indeed I knew him, why not? He was my class-fellow. He used to live in the same mohalla as I did. That bullock cart by which he had gone to Paro's village, is still there at the back of my house. Do go and have a look at it some time…stupid girl…!"

He turned with a violent jerk and opened the door. He then shut it quickly, and racing down the stairs, disappeared like a gust of air.

That stupid girl stood there with her mouth agape…

It seemed Deep Di had just come after her bath. Big transparent drops of water were sliding down to the points of her hair spreading over her back. Her well-formed, shapely body wrapped in a saree, white as milk-froth…her body emitting a kind of fragrance.

Her lips, soft as silk, parted. It was as though some pearls were scattered. Deep Di seemed glad about his coming. Still, she looked at him with mock anger…

"Why didn't you come sooner?"

"I did…"

"You did!" she said with a grimace." I have kept the breakfast ready since morning. Just look, I haven't even had my tea." Leaning against the table, she half-sat at its edge. Then she gave him an intent look." You haven't combed your hair this morning. Nor have you washed your face…Did you go to study straight from…your bed?... A pigeon that you are!"

He couldn't say anything. He felt crushed by the intimacy shown by Deep Di… It pleased him greatly when Deep Di called him "pigeon" in anger.

"Now, why are you sitting there like a guest?" She said petulantly after a brief silence. "Go to the bathroom. I've kept some hot water there. In the meantime, I shall boil some more water for tea. The water I had set to boil has gone black- it has been boiling for three hours…"

Saket quietly got up like a domesticated animal and entered the bathroom. A washed towel hung on a peg. A silken hair was sticking to a wet cake of sandalwood soap. Steam rose up like smoke from a brass bucket.

He felt really light and refreshed after bathing with no further ado. It seemed as though a great weight had gone from his body.

Now his mood was somewhat changed. Wrapping Deep Di's coloured saree like a lungi he stood before Deep Di's dressing table. He delicately poured the fragrant oil from Deep Di's surahi-shaped bottle on his palm. He brought his palm close to his nose before applying that oil to his hair…then he combed his hair with Deep Di's big nylon comb. He was astounded and also somewhat pleased to see his reflection in Deep Di's full-sized mirror. He felt a kind of self-satisfaction he hadn't felt before.

Deep Di spread a colourful plastic tablecloth and quickly started laying the table. Holding three or four spoons in her hand, she brought a metal plate as though it had been prepared for aarati. Pouring the tea very stylishly from the kettle into the cups, she asked: "Did you have your dinner last night?"

Deep Di appeared to be in low spirits but her eyes were fixed steadily on the catechu-coloured stream.

"Yes."

"Yes, you're saying? You enjoy telling lies!" She went on without looking at him. "Your face tells me you haven't had a meal for at least a hundred years."

Saket just smiled.

"What else does my face tell you?" He gave her a mischievous look after a brief pause.

"Only that..." Deep Di looked around for the milk pot. She removed the extra utensils lying on the table and kept them on the teapoy. Then she rose again and muttered as if talking to herself:

"Only that you're a liar. You're careless. But does one's face ever tell a lie? Bet for a lakh of rupees if you don't believe me... O.K.? What are you thinking now?"

Saket burst out laughing. "If I had one lakh, wouldn't I get married?"

"Why?" Deep Di continued talking to him as she clanged the vessels and rattled the spoons. "Can't you marry if you had ninety thousand? Why not?"

"Ninety thousand would spell ruin," he said and laughed at his own words. Deep Di liked to see him laugh like that. "Arrey, will you simply go on laughing with folded hands or will you do justice to these things?"

Saket was really hungry. He quickly stuffed one slice after the other in his mouth.

Deep Di took a large sip of her tea.

"I say, eat slowly! Is it running away or what?" Deep Di asked angrily and Saket smiled.

"You look very charming when you're angry, Deep Di!"

Deep Di gave him an intent look. "You've become very naughty, I say! Well, now tell me, why didn't you eat yesterday?"

"Just like that! Isn't there a food shortage in the country? I thought I might as well help a bit in solving the food problem!"

"So, You're out to solve the food problem, is it?" Deep Di muttered and draining the remaining tea in the cup into a used glass, prepared a fresh cup of tea.

"When do your exams begin?"

"From the 6th of April."

"You'll be at the top this time too, won't you?"

"It's difficult!" he said, nibbling at a biscuit like a squirrel. "I don't know what's gone wrong. I keep forgetting things very soon... I can't remember anything, however much I try."

Deep Di remained silent for a while, lost in thought. Then breaking the silence she said softly: "Why don't you eat almonds? They say almonds improve memory."

Saket became suddenly grim: "Indeed, you're right." And then leaving a sigh he continued: "I'm planning to practise Picking Pockets for a few months — it would solve one of my life's major problems."

"Arrey!" Deep Di was astounded. "You mean to say you can't afford even two almonds a day?"

"Why not?" Saket kept his cup at the empty side of the table. "My digestive system is very good, Deep Di! Why two, I can take ten almonds a day. You've said the right thing, I shall note it down in my diary today."

Soft notes of music could be heard. A radio was on in the back room. Both of them nibbled the rest of their breakfast in silence. There was no communication between them.

Deep Di wanted to prepare more tea but Saket shook his head and stopped her. She stretched her limbs and got up. Putting the cups on the tray, she went inside. Saket leaned against the back of the sofa and while reading the newspaper, closed his eyes.

She tip-toed back into the room, took the remaining utensils and kept them under the running water of the tap.

She wiped the table, washed her hands with soap, and wiping her face with the pallu of her saree, came back to the drawing room with the intention of sitting there for a few moments.

"I say, you've really gone to sleep!"

He remained in the same position — still and unmoved!

She came close to him, moved still closer and stood almost touching him. She stroked his hair which was dishevelled by the wind.

"I say, your hair has turned so grey!"

THREE

The morning fog gradually lifted, Saket was standing on the verandah — looking worried. Gusts of chilly wind were violently shaking the branches of eucalyptus trees. Saket was shivering a bit. Deep Di switched off the radio. Sitting on the floor, she was marking the test papers of her college.

Saket couldn't decide what he should do. To how many people should he narrate the same thing over again? He himself didn't like doing that. Even otherwise, he was very hesitant by nature. However much he tried, he wouldn't be able to open his mouth. It was more than two months and he hadn't yet received the three hundred and twenty-five rupees of his scholarship. He was expecting something from Major Verma, but... He didn't feel like going to Dada Babu's place. If Dada Babu started narrating his usual story, he would have to be there till evening. Even last evening... Saket could see no way out.

"Why don't you sit and be at ease? What are you thinking, standing with your hand on your forehead?" Deep Di asked.

Saket didn't hear her as it were.

"Arrey, I'm going to cook. What have you been thinking carrying that heavy coat?" Deep Di said as she put aside the notebooks.

The coat continued to hang on Saket's arms like a dead kite.

There was silence for a while. Deep Di got up, leaving the notebooks spread on the floor. There were wrinkles not only in her saree but also on her forehead.

Deep Di snatched that heavy coat from his lowered arms.

"What has happened to you? I'm scared to look at your face!"

Saket's eyes remained fixed in a void as it were.

"See, you've put me in a fix. I can't do engineering or any such thing." He looked at Deep Di.

"Why, why?"

"Just like that!" he held Deep Di's arms and shook her impulsively. "Can't get me some sort of job in your own college?"

Deep Di raised her eyes. His hands remained where they were.

"Just tell me yourself, how can I do all that?"

Deep Di gazed at him: "It's a matter of just two years!"

"You're talking about two years while..." he raised his voice and then stopped short.

"Then would something happen if you lose heart? You're a man and look at the way you're talking" Deep Di said petulantly. But Saket kept his palm on her lips.

"Enough! Don't give me a sermon. I don't need any advice... I don't need it", he almost shrieked, shaking his head. Deep Di felt pressure on her amis. He snatched the coat from her and running down the stairs, vanished out of sight.

Major Verma had gone to Shimla to see the snow. An aged barber was busy cutting the hair of a child seated between the two armrests of a chair in Dada Babu's shop.

Dada Babu had piled up lots of vegetables on his small push-cart. Pushing it with both hands, he turned slowly at the bend of the road.

Saket was very depressed. He wanted to meet Dada Babu, but when he saw him, he couldn't bear to look at him. He quickly rushed past him.

"I say, you engineer-to-be! Engineer Babu!"

Saket really couldn't hear him. Hanging the coat over his shoulders, he walked with heavy steps, like a corpse. He would have certainly met Rasan if he came over. Bishan Das had promised to pay the arrears of the tuition money at his house. But it wasn't Tuesday today.

When he reached the threshold of the house, he woke up from his dream. He raised his head and found Roop seated on the stairs stitching something.

"You're very late today, Bhaiya!"

"Hmm," Saket threw his coat at her.

"Ma has kept the food ready for long now."

"Hmm, she has cooked? Where did she get the rations from? He pursed his lips.

"Arrey, you yourself sent the rations — Have you forgotten?"

"I... did I send the rations?"

"Of course, this morning. The servant from the lady in our neighbourhood had come."

"Which lady?"

"That one, who's teaching in the college. Deepa Bhanji!" That servant said, "Babu has sent. He was getting late for his tuition!"

"Oh, I see...!" he shook his head. Going up the stairs in long strides he opened the door and his eyes opened wide at the sight of the house.

The utensils lay in a heap. The vessel of daal was upturned and rice was scattered all over. Chhoti Ma was beating the children ruthlessly. The clothes on her body were in shreds.

Chhoti Ma probably had another attack. It had been going on like that for the past three years — one couldn't predict what would happen.

Chhaya lay crouched in a corner. Her closed fists were soiled with rice and daal. Some grains of rice had got stuck to her mouth.

The moment she heard Saket's voice, she came close to him. She held his legs by encircling her arms around them. That left yellowish marks of soiled hands on Saket's pants.

He opened the door and silently went to his room.

He dropped himself listlessly on his bed, face downwards — like a broker pillar.

Suddenly heard someone walking stealthily like a cat.

Two tiny hands groped and touched him.

"Dadda, have you gone to sleep?"

Saket, lying there with his eyes closed, gathered her in his arms.

"Did you eat anything?"

"NO."

"...!"

"Won't you have a meal, Dadda ?"

"...!"

"Stretch out your fingers — I'll count and tell you if it's one finger or two. I can't see anything now, Dadda!"

The drawing of a bridge on paper — Saket felt that the bridge had grown too big. With the point of his pen, he destroyed that bridge bit by bit. Then he drew another bridge with a building looming over it. The building was so big that its other end was not visible. He tried to draw a picture of a dam by its side with criss-cross lines.

Then, out of irritation, he destroyed all that and turned the next page. A thick, crooked line developed into a map of India... On the right edge, some drops of ink had been sprayed, resembling some islands. On one such island, he thought, his father must have passed his last days.

That morning there was a letter from his maternal uncle informing him about some government scheme for the benefit of political sufferers.

"Hmm!" Saket smiled ironically, and thinking something to himself, became silent.

He crumpled the paper into a little ball and pressed it in his hand for a long time. Then he suddenly got up with a jerk. He saw a little sparrow pecking at the grain. For no reason, he took aim at the bird. The bird flew away with a sudden flutter and sat on the branch of a nearby tree. In between, it moved its neck from side to side in panic and tried to peck the grains with its bill again.

Saket put on his slippers and went out. He had hardly walked a hundred feet when he heard a voice, at the end of the lane:

"Engineer Babu…"

The coat Saket had casually thrown over the shoulder, still hung there. He asked: "Who's it — Dada Babu?"

"My dear Engineer, just tell me how does one sell vegetables?" All the vegetables I brought from the mandi in the morning are lying unsold."

Saket walked up to him and started checking the vegetables. "Indeed, they're all fresh!"

"Oh, they're absolutely fresh. Imagine that they're not on this push-cart but in the field..."

"What's your price for potatoes?"

"Two rupees a seer."

"Karela?"

"Two fifty a seer."

"Brinjal"

"Three and a half rupees."

"Pumpkin?"

"Pumpkin is six rupees a seer."

Dada Babu looked at the pumpkin and then at Saket's round face. He said: "My rates are fixed, Engineer Babu. The bigger the size of the vegetable the higher the price!"

Saket smiled: "How much have you sold since morning?"

Dada Babu took out the money from his cap, which served the purpose of a money bag. "The Goddess Lakshmi has graced me with the earning of seven and a quarter annas."

Saket picked up a small ripe tomato and put it in his mouth like a rasagulla and asked: "What happened to your paan shop, Dada Babu?"

"The wretched business went into a big loss," the flaccid Dada Babu replied.

"Sell your vegetables at cheaper rates, Dada Babu. Who the devil would think of buying a pumpkin at six rupees a seer?"

"You won't understand, Engineer. There's a world of a difference between building bridge and selling vegetables," Dada Babu observed. He kept the money from the cap under the weighing scale and put the cap on his head.

Saket held a couple of potatoes in his hand. He went on to sing and catch them.

"Sir, what's the price of potatoes?"

Saket looked around in confusion. Major Verma's daughter who looked like a camel, stood there with a plastic basket in hand.

"You sell vegetables too, Sir!"

"Yes, I not only sell vegetables, I also cut grass!"

"How does cutting the grass help, Sir?"

Saket fell silent— maybe he wasn't able to hear properly.

"Sir, Aunty said in the school today that we're all descendants of apes."

Saket put one more tomato in his mouth. He made a face like an ape and gazed at her, shaking his head.

"Your aunt was indeed right — we actually are the descendants of apes, there's no doubt about it. What do you say, Dada Babu?"

He gave a thud on Dada Babu's bald head, and hanging his coat on his shoulder, turned and walked away…

The day had just dawned. A flock of birds flew over his head creating a picturesque sight. Then there was an uninterrupted flow of buses, scooters and cars. The cold gusty wind ruthlessly scathed the body. Saket had wrapped his khadi coat tight around his body. Both his arms were covered. The flocks of cotton had stuck to his ears, mouth head, hands — all over the body. Even the hair on his head appeared white with it.

Trying to avoid being seen, he walked very fast. His speed increased as he passed Deep Di's house so that no one would notice him.

As he was about to pass the pavement lined with eucalyptus trees, he actually heard Deep Di calling out: "Saket!"

He walked up and stood hesitantly before her as if he were in a dilemma.

"You're walking barefoot so early in the morning! What are you doing?"

"It's on doctor's instructions," Deep explained. "But where are you going so early in the morning looking like a monkey?"

Saket said in the same serious tone: "Doctor has given the same instruction to me, Deep Di."

He smiled and so did Deep.

"What is that bundle tucked under your armpit, eh?"

He kept the packet on an iron bench in front of them. He took out one item after the other from it and said: " This is the medicine for Chhaya's eyes. These fruits are for my mother. This saree is for Roop." And he burst into laughter. Then he suddenly grew serious: "Anni had been going to school without wearing shoes for the past month. Deep Di, what all things they long to have! They're still children — children!"

Deep Di looked on with curiosity.

"But from where are you coming in this clumsy attire?"

Moistening the lips with his tongue he rested one foot on the bench and said: "You know, Rattan —-our Rattan! I've started doing the night shift with him in a hosiery. I've been going there regularly for five days. I get paid according to the work I put in!" He produced before her a few crumpled old currency notes.

"Haven't you brought anything for me?"

"Don't I myself belong to you, Deep Di?" He gazed at Deep Di very innocently. Such unspoilt, innocent expression always pleased Deep Di. She gazed at him without batting her eyelids — hypnotized as it were.

"I should take your leave. I must go for my tuition at half past six."

"Drop in at my place on your way there. I shall keep tea ready for you."

"Just tea?" He laughed. "Nothing for breakfast?" He looked back and gave her an intent look.

Deep Di kept gazing at him till he disappeared in a cluster of trees…

"You were very dejected the other day. I was almost wondering if you would start going up the Qutub Minar!!"

"That's life Deep Di! In fact, I had the same thought in my mind. But then I said to myself — 'If I've got to die, why not die after climbing Everest? What's so very great about going up the Qutub Minar…?'"

Saket had worn a washed shirt and tight-fitting pants. His shoes too had a shine. He looked very smart.

"Now, now... where did you disappear all these days, engineer saheb? You weren't seen anywhere!"

"You can see me now!" Saket said with a little sarcasm. "Don't walk too much on the grass in the morning hours — otherwise, you'll start writing poems!"

Deep Di pursed her lips and smiled to herself.

"Now, will you give me something to eat or go on with your melodrama? It's almost a quarter past six."

Deep Di brought the breakfast and quickly laid the table as though it was a tea stall — so many utensils?

Before she would bring tea, he applied a thick layer of butter on his toast with a knife. Deep simply gazed at him.

"You'll polish off all that butter, is it?"

Saket's mouth was so full, both his cheeks had puffed up. Chewing the toast hurriedly, he said:" You know that girl, Major Verma's daughter? She really pesters me so much! That stupid girl, she's like a camel. She can't pass her examination even in a hundred years."

He finished eating in a great hurry and after downing three cups of tea, got ready to leave. He wiped the butter on his lips with the pallu of Deep Di's saree. When Deep got offended, he simply laughed — to irritate her.

"Had it been like the old times, you would have slapped me, isn't it?"

Deep Di remained silent.

"What are you thinking?" He asked.

"Nothing."

"You're thinking of something!"

"Now swot, I say! you're getting delayed."

He walked a few steps and then came back. "We shall go shopping. Keep yourself dressed and ready. We'll have coffee in a nice restaurant. And this time, it's on me, yes!"

Saket went away. Deep sat thinking about 'something...'

Deep Di was very cheerful and happy all through the day. She herself could not understand why. She didn't get angry with anyone. She went about chirping the whole day.

In the evening, she started dressing up at the appointed time. Which saree should she wear? She couldn't make up her mind. She pulled out all her sarees but didn't like any of them. Ultimately, she selected a white dacron saree and a white blouse, and also white sandals.

She didn't realize how long she had been standing before the mirror in various dancing poses and slants. She repeatedly stroked her own face, rubbing the wrinkles with her fingers. 'She didn't want to give the impression that she was old, so very old.

When Saket arrived at a quarter past six, he found Deep Di standing in the balcony — weather lost in the depths of the past or the future, none could say.

Saket entered the room whistling. Then looking at Deep Di he hesitated for a moment.

"I can't even recognize you today, Deep Di!"

Deep Di stood somewhat abashed.

"We shall take the umbrella with us, won't we? It's bound to rain today."

He laughed. Deep Di also spontaneously laughed the same laugh.

"You're looking just like a foreigner. Deep Di! I had never imagined you could be so charming." He smiled again and then laughed and then looked at Deep Di!

Deep Di was really abashed. She said: "Now, stop it, will you? At times you really act like a small baby....!"

Saket dumped himself on the sofa — dangling his feet in front of the sofa and stretching his arms far at the back.

"Are we not going?" Deep Di asked, swinging her handbag.

"We shall go in our time. Who's waiting for us there?"

"Then won't it get late?"

"Of course, it would," Saket said, stretching his limbs. "All right. Let me have something to drink and eat."

Deep Di brought a glass of water.

"Tch! Only water! Nothing to eat?"

"Now will you only talk about eating or start moving?" Deep Di said with irritation. "Once your stomach is full, you'll say you're feeling sleepy and can't walk! I really don't know how you'll ever become an engineer!"

Saket emptied that glass of water in a single gulp and stood up wiping his lips with a handkerchief.

"Well, let's go. We shall eat something in the restaurant. Come what may, you would see to it that I do become an engineer!"

They came out on the road.

"Where have you left your coat today?"

"Oh, didn't I tell you? Roop just soaked it in water. She said that when it is washed, the Yamuna would become dark once again. Something similar must have happened even in satyug — some sage must have washed his old garments so that the colour of the poor Yamuna must have changed and became dark!"

Deep Di started laughing.

"You're wearing just a shirt — won't you feel cold?"

Saket appeared to be looking somewhere else.

"The sweater I am knitting will be ready in a couple of days."

They kept walking in silence. Somebody, passing by on a scooter, waved at him but he didn't see.

"Isn't it a little chillier today?"

"Right, I do feel a little cold." Deep Di touched his shirt to judge how cold it was.

"How many hours are you required to put in at the hosiery?"

"Abut six hours."

"How many tuitions are you giving?"

"The same as before."

"What about your studies?"

"Yes, I'm proceeding at the speed of a turtle and I do study a bit."

"You work so hard from morning till evening. When do you sleep?"

"Well, I doze a little while eating, a little while walking, a little while reading."

Saket started at Deep Di and said: "Why are you glaring at me like that? Am I saying anything wrong?..."

They came to the main market. The place was beginning to get more crowded. People were rubbing shoulders with one another. The glare of neon-lights glided down to the roads.

"Shall be a little impertinent?"

Deep Di probably couldn't understand him.

"Just see that flower-seller-he has been following you pleading…please buy a string of flowers — he too should have his evening bread."

Deep Di couldn't refuse. She took out a string of fresh, half-blossomed flowers from the basket. When she started fumbling in her handbag, Saket caught her hand. "Please, would you mind if I pay?"

Saket paid without bargaining for the amount the flower-seller asked for.

"I hope you didn't feel upset, Deep Di?" They started walking on the pavement a little removed from the crowd.

He had expected Deep Di to say something. But she said nothing in response.

The restaurant was full. There was no place to sit. They stood waiting for some time and then, as they were about to leave the restaurant, one of the bearers in a black coat indicated that there was an unoccupied table on the balcony and they could sit there if they had no objection.

Both of them were quite tired. Without a word, they started following the bearer.

It was a cabin which resembled a dark box. Hesitatingly, they slumped on the soft chairs.

The bearer brought two glasses of cold water and giving them the menu card, waited in silence.

Saket turned the pages of the menu card and asked: "What will you have with coffee?"

"Only espresso coffee."

Saket looked at the bearer without saying anything.

FOUR

It was a seclusion to which they were not accustomed. They found it quite odd. Since the silence was becoming oppressive, Saket said, for the sake of saying: "Where will you spend your holidays this year?"

"Nowhere, Saket. I have no desire to go anywhere."

"Don't you get bored with this loneliness at times?"

"What does one gain by getting bored?"

"Why don't you settle down to a married life?"

Deep Di yawned and said: "Very well, since you're saying it. But it seems to me that I'm all right as I am free of all that bother. I've lived all my life like this — the rest of it would also be similarly spent...! A solitary being that I am, why should I go in for all that trouble?"

"Don't your family people insist?" He said, breaking that silence.

"Who's left in the family in any case? My parents, who were anxious about me, are dead. My brothers are so busy they've no time at all. In the world of today, who ever bothers to think about anyone else?"

Coffee was brought and they started sipping it.

"Why have you hidden away that string of jasmine flowers in your purse? It would wither away, poor thing! Put it in your hair. It would look very nice."

Deep Di took out the string of flowers from her handbag and tucked it in her hair carelessly.

"Oh, not like that, Deep Di. Tuck it a little sideways. It's a new fashion these days."

Deep Di did as he said.

"Now you're really looking more beautiful than ever, Deep Di!" Though offended, Deep Di smiled.

They finished drinking their coffee.

Saket was adamant and paid the bill. Then looking at the watch he said: "Oh, it's time already. May I take your leave now?"

"Arrey, you can go after a while. Won't you drop me at home?"

Saket couldn't refuse her although he was getting late, and he went with Deep Di.

"Let's sit in the park for a while! You won't get late, would you?" Deep Di gave him a questioning look. "I like to sit on lush green grass in the darkening evening."

Saket gave Deep Di a confused look.

"Come on, let's sit for a little while! I don't come out with you every day, do I?" She held Saket's hand affectionately and as a matter of right, started going towards the park without waiting for his reaction.

They sat at the far end of the park.

"Saket, what are you thinking at this moment?"

"Nothing at all!"

"Don't you feel lonely at times?"

"Where do I have time for such feelings ?" Saket replied somewhat dejectedly.

"I am really very troubled at times. And at such moments, there's nothing I can do. I have read and cast away hundreds of books, I also did gardening as a hobby and started several activities at the same time. But in the end, 1 found myself in the same spot...." and she heaved a deep sigh.

Saket remained silent.

"Just see how my forehead is hot today!" and as she leaned forward. Saket touched her forehead with his fingers.

"Are you sure you aren't running a fever?"

"Oh, no, at times I just feel heavy like this."

They sat silent for a few moments.

"Come. I'll take you home. There's already dew in the air. See our clothes have become damp already."

He helped Deep Di rise to her feet. She was truly unwell. He engaged a scooter. Deep Di rested her head on his shoulder

Saket was having his meal. Roop stood before him with a glass of water Chayya sat on the edge of the bed, dangling her legs. Anni had stood first in his class. He was eating from the same plate as Saket, nudging close to him.

"Roop, are you never in need of money or anything else? Why don't you ask for something?" Saket asked her breaking a piece of roti.

"I have got everything, Bhaiya! What should I do with money? I'm not a child!"

"Now, now! You're already grown big, is it?" He laughed for no reason "I don't know what all the children of your age wear and what all they eat! And how much they spend! Only you, like an old woman, keep stitching old and torn kameez..." He suddenly stopped midway.

After a while, he remembered something as it were: "Arrey, haven't you bought a saree for yourself?"

"I've got sarees. What's the point of unnecessarily piling up clothes?"

She was about to say something more but Anni suddenly said: "Didi has bought a shirt-piece for you, Bhaiya!"

"Why, why have you brought it for me?" He looked questioningly at Roop.

"Then will you go around in the same torn shirt? What would people think?"

"Oh, if you start worrying about what people say, then you're done for. People may say anything. Why should we bother?"

Roop brought some more rotis and put them in Saket's plate per force.

"Again you've forced me to overeat today! Now I'll feel sleepy and my work will suffer!" and then he asked as though he had suddenly remembered: "And yes, how is Ma's health? Has she taken her meal?"

"Yes!"

"Did you give her the medicine?"

"She refused to take it... In the morning, she washed the logs of wood and tried to light them in the chulha. When the logs didn't burn, she just poured water in the chulha. She threw around utensils and tore Anni's new shirt into shreds. When Anni started crying, she beat him up ruthlessly."

Saket continued eating in silence. He then dipped his fingers in the glass and cleaned his mouth.

"I shall have a new shirt made for you, right?"

Anni, almost in tears, nodded his head.

"Chhaya has become dumb, isn't it, Roop?" Saket said looking at Chhaya, who was seated on the side. "I'm told she doesn't talk at all."

"She talks a lot, Dadda!" Anni remarked. "She moves her mouth like a goat the whole day. I don't know why she becomes silent the moment she sees you!"

"Keep quiet, will you? You're a great one to complain, stupid!"

Saket lifted Chhaya and made her sit by his side.

"Have you put medicine in your eyes?"

She just nodded her head to say, "Yes."

"Does Roop beat you?"

"No."

"Are you able to see anything?"

"A little."

"All right. Now tell me, what's there on the opposite wall?"

Chhaya looked hard at the wall and said: "There's a photak (photo).

"Whose photak?"

"Of the bearded Baba."

Roop and Anni burst out laughing at the same time.

"Bearded Baba! Arrey, don't you recognize Father's photo?"

Chhaya felt embarrassed.

"Where's Father, Bhaiya?" Anni asked, thinking something.

"There's a beautiful place called heaven, where innumerable Gods live. Father lives there with those Gods."

"But why doesn't he come here sometimes?"

"Arrey, do people ever come back from there!" Roop said, pitying him for meagre intelligence.

"If so, let's go there ourselves. Father will be very happy to see us."

They all burst into loud guffaws.

How quickly time passes! Saket just didn't realize how the last five years had gone by... He was seated on the sand on the river bank — heaping up sand with both his hands. Occasionally, he straightened his fingers in the process of smearing what he wrote and sometimes made some baffling patterns in the sand.

Deep Di was seated close to him. She had dipped both her feet in the water, and gathering her saree up to the knees, had been throwing pebbles in the water.

"When will your result be out, Saket?" She addressed the question as though to herself.

"Any day, now. But why are you asking?"

"Just like that."

Saket got up shaking off the hands from his clothes and sat next to Deep Di dipping both his bare feet in the water. Like Deep Di, he too collected a heap of pebbles and went on taking aims on the waves.

"What do you plan to do after the results are declared?"

"Whatever you say."

"I was wondering whether you would get a job somewhere?"

"Why not? But that's not in our hands, is it?"

"Right you are!" Deep Di said with a sigh. "What do we have in our hands, in any case? Like the strings of puppets, we continue to live day after day...!" She suddenly fell silent.

The waves dashing on the bank and a deep silence... The darkness grew thicker all around. Deep Di could not bear that terrible silence.

"What are you thinking, Saket?"

"Nothing... Just..."

Deep Di took water in her cupped hands and then let it fall.

"I was thinking, Deep Di....!" Saket muttered and stopped midway.

Deep Di looked at him eagerly. She said: "What is it?"

"Nothing. Just some absurd thoughts..." Then he changed the course of the conversation. "See, that corpse burning there!"

Deep Di also started looking in that direction. The reflections of the leaping flames in the water... as though water were on fire and the waves were flaring up like oil...

A boat passed cutting through the waves.

Deep Di started at the boat like an excited young child.

"Why don't you think about your future?" he asked.

"What should I think?"

Saket removed his wet feet from the water and after wiping them with his handkerchief, rested them on a slightly wet stone...

Deep Di withdrew her feet too and wiped the cold hands with the end of her saree. Then bending over the waves and taking water in her cupped hands, washed her face. She enjoyed the cool touch of water on her face. Saket, sitting by her side, was staring at something in the sky...

"Come on let's go!" He pulled up Deep Di by holding her hand.

They walked side by side, their feet sinking into the sand.

"It would be nice if I pass the examination and get some job here itself... I was thinking that if that happened, I would get a nice house which you too could share with us... for whom do you have to do this job... you too would live as we are living..."

Deep Di said with a deep sigh: "If you dream too much, you become more miserable. Life should be allowed to go along its own course. What do you think?"

Saket did not answer that question...

Dada Babu's push-cart on which he loaded the vegetables had been confiscated by the municipal corporation. After that Saket got him a job in his hosiery mill. He now sold banians. "The bigger the banian, the higher the price" — Dada Babu still followed his favourite rule of trade. He carried a pile of banians on his shoulder and hawked them from street to street.

In the evening he came to Saket and handed over to him the daily sales proceeds.

"Engineer Babu, is there at least some little money left in balance?"

Saket placed in his hands the balance of some two rupees. He said: "Put in more effort, Dada Babu! How can you carry on unless you have for yourself five or six rupees after going round the town the whole day?"

"When you become an engineer, have a machine under your control. Then see if I don't earn a hundred or even more every day...!"

Saket laughed at Dada Babu's talk...

Since last year, Saket had started giving tuition to children on a large scale. He had been calling all children at his own house and teaching them all at the same time. As a result, he earned so much money that he was able to meet all expenses quite easily.

He also made his modest contribution to the treatment of Rattan's mother. There was also some improvement in Chhaya's eyes. He bought a saree for Deep Di with the money he had saved during the previous months. And Roop was not found stitching torn clothes any more.

But Saket had an overgrowth of hair and his clothes were as clumsy as ever. Where did he have time to attend to those things?

Chhoti Ma did not get frequent attacks of her illness as before. But she had turned more religious. If she so much as caught a glimpse of somebody's face before her puja, she promptly bathed again. She bathed exactly twenty-one times a day. She didn't have her meals in the evening. She never allowed anyone to enter the puja room and the kitchen. She cleaned with her own hands the already cleaned utensils all over again.

If someone ever entered a room with shoes on, she swept the floor with cow dung that very moment. She did not take her lunch unless she had fed the cow with the apportioned share and had a glimpse of the Sun God. She had stitched dresses for the idols of the Gods with her own hands. She bathed those idols every day and dressed them up. At lunchtime, she placed before those idols food by way of offering. She took her lunch only after that routine was over. After lunch, she put her Gods to sleep so that they rested during the day, and then she would go for her afternoon sleep. For her Gods, she had made a tiny little bed with a silk cushion on which they were laid for their night's sleep after dinner. The tiny cups and bowls — all the utensils meant for the Gods in fact — were kept apart and nobody could ever touch them without bathing first.

Roop often said lightly: "Bhaiya, bring a small transistor for these Gods so that they can get the news from heaven…!"

The sun hadn't risen yet. Darkness had somewhat lifted. The birds perched on the branches of the tree were chirping vigorously. Saket came out of the hosiery and enjoyed the free air outside and the serene atmosphere of the morning.

Cotton flocks were stuck all over his body, clothes, and hair. His overgrown beard was covered with white patches, which gave Saket's innocent face a very strange appearance.

His coat hung at his shoulder as usual. He whistled as he walked with long strides.

He came to the road junction and noticed a big crowd. People were pouncing upon newspapers like kites. There was such an uproar.

Saket's steps came to a sudden halt. He remembered it was the 17th of the month — perhaps the results of his examination were out.

He also swooped on a newspaper: "Just see please, if the results of the engineering examination are announced."

A youth who had failed gave him a tearful look.

Saket made a wry face.

He moved towards another group of people who were swarming like ants. Slowly making his way through the crowd he reached right in the middle.

"Yes, yes! yes, I say... what did you say, please..." With a jerk, he turned the page of the newspaper, with its one end left in another man's hand...

"Engineering!" he shouted aloud. He could not believe his eyes when he saw his own name printed on the top.

"Please see, Babuji — it's really Saket, isn't it?"

A Bengali Babu looked closely through his thick glasses and said: "Yes, yes, it should be Saket."

"Should it be Saket?" asked Saket with a strange vein.

Saket jumped before that Bengali gentleman could nod his heavy head... He tossed the newspaper and cried: "Should be Saket... Saket!"

He crumpled the newspaper and tossed it in the air and then caught it in his hands. Like a charging bull, he started storming through the crowd when somebody tugged at the sleeve of his coat: "That newspaper is mine…"

Saket pulled the coat to himself with a jerk saying: "It's mine."

His old coat could not stand that violent jerk. The sleeve of the coat remained in that Bengali Babu's hand. But Saket was in no mood to look back. Oblivious to the surroundings, he ran, with the newspaper flying in the air like a kite.

Some children ran after him raising loud cries. But he ran on straight.

Deep Di was walking barefoot on the grass. Saket went up to the lawn, jumping over the wall like a monkey, and waving the torn newspaper in the air shouted: "I'm made!"

Holding Deep Di tight in his arms, he swung her around three or four times.

Deep Di got scared: "I say, what's the matter? Will you say something or...?" Looking on with embarrassment at the people standing on their balconies, die tried to disengage herself. "Arrey, have you gone crazy? See, people are looking at us! What will they think?"

"Saket got to pass?" As he tried to show her the newspaper he had been crushing in his hand he realized what he had done. What was left in his hand was just a small piece of paper — the rest had vanished.

He spread out that bit of paper to show her — but it was only the torn advertisement of monkey brand tooth powder!

"Arrey, what are you seeing in this? First class first — give me your hand!" he forcibly grabbed Deep Di's hand.

"Are you telling the truth?"

"Then you think it's not true, is it?"

Deep Di's eyes opened wide, very wide with joy.

"What are you staring at in my face? Will you give me sweets or simply…!"

He sat on the wall — looking like a langoor, with all those flocks of cotton sticking all over his body.

"You'll feed me with a platter full of sweets with your own hands. If my mouth cannot take all those sweets, you'll have to stuff them in your own mouth. You'll have to chew and swallow them on my behalf."

Deep Di's face glowed like the flame of a lamp.

"I say, you've really crossed the sea as it were!" Deep Di's voice choked. Picking up his torn coat, she led him inside. Like an innocent child, she wiped his face with a wet cloth and cleaned off the cotton floss.

"So, the morning dream has come true! I dreamt yesterday that you were crossing the sea by a boat all by yourself."

Saket was so happy that he could not sit still. He would get up every few minutes, then sit again and look around uneasily.

When he got up to leave, Deep Di stopped him: "Where are you rushing without even taking tea? You must have worked the whole night. Aren't you tired?"

"I can't tell you how tired I was. But that tired feeling has vanished like camphor in the air..." He then turned round and said: "I'll be back in a short while. You make tea in the meantime."

He went down the stairs but returned immediately. He said: "Didi, where have you kept my coat? I can't walk unless I have that coat on my shoulder."

Deep Di looked at him with a smile: "That torn coat without the sleeves? What would people say if they saw it?"

"Don't say that, Didi. Please let me have it," he pleaded. Deep Di just shook her head without saying anything.

Saket waited for a moment and then left, cutting a sorry figure.

FIVE

He rushed straight to Chhoti Ma's room, who was picking flowers for her puja after bathing. She gave him a startled look and Saket burst out laughing.

"Your puja has borne fruit, Amma! I've passed the examination." Venomous words of abuse remained stuck in Chhoti Ma's mouth.

"Didn't I say, Bhaiya, that you would surely stand first?" Roop's face had an unusual glow.

Chhaya got up from her bed and groped her way towards Saket and held him tight at his knees with both her hands.

Sick though she was, Rattan's mother arrived in the evening. She stroked Saket's face with her hands. She said: "Good deeds of parents do bear fruits one day or the other. Your mother was so good-hearted! And your father was not a man, but a God in himself. There will be no dharma left in the world if the children of such good parents have to live in hardship…" and the old woman's eyes filled with tears.

Mr. Verma, who went every winter to see the snow, invited him for tea at his house. He was astonished, but happy that a boy like him had broken the university record…

Mr. Verma congratulated him and made him sit by his side: "Wonderful, my boy! Your professor Dr. Majumdar said that he had not seen another student like you in his life. God willing, you would be the only engineer of your kind. Only one in a million would have a fertile brain like yours."

Mr. Verma's camel-like stupid daughter brought the snacks. "Sir, how does a record get broken?" She asked as she sat on a chair.

Saket didn't say anything at first, but in the end, he had to speak because she went on asking persistently. "When you drop a record on the floor it automatically breaks," he said.

"Ho! Ho!" Mr. Verma laughed hysterically. "Original idea!"

"Do you build bridges, Sir? But you were selling potatoes on the road that day."

Saket laughed and shook his head.

"What happens by shaking the head, Sir?"

"Nothing!" he replied nonchalantly.

"Sometimes I sell potatoes and sometimes build bridges." Everyone laughed. Seeing all of them laugh, the girl also laughed…

Deep Di had made tea long ago and was waiting. She leaned out of the window and looked out and then sat on the sofa stretching her hands and legs full length and closing her eyes.

Suddenly, there was a sound of steps on the stairs. She got up at once and opened the door. It was the newspaper boy standing there with the bill…

At about a quarter past ten, Saket noisily walked up the same stairs. Deep Di had rested her head on her knees, as though absolutely unaware of his arrival.

"Have you gone to sleep?" he said as he stealthily walked in.

Deep Di's dry hair fluttered in the breeze of the fan. Saket sat down silently and stroked Deep Di's dishevelled hair, straightened the folded end of her saree, and drew in her hands stretching before the sofa.

"Are you really offended, Deep Di?" He gave her a childlike look. "Won't you talk to me?"

She didn't reply.

"Really — you won't talk?"

He lifted Deep Di's head affectionately and said: "Tehh ... you're crying, Deep Di!"

Deep Di's eyes were an odd expression.

There was silence in the air for a while.

"Does one get offended over such a triviality? I did remember that you would have made tea and would be waiting.... that you wouldn't have taken your tea... you would be looking out from the balcony every now and then... But I was so caught up among the people that..."

Deep Di hid her head in his lap and wept bitterly like a small child.

Saket didn't say anything and pressed his head on Deep Di's bent head.

There was silence in the room — except for the whirling sound of the fan.

"Now get up! Don't you have to go to college today?"

He held Deep Di's face in both his palms and said: "I too haven't had tea since morning."

Deep Di got up reluctantly. She wiped her face with the end of her saree and adjusted her dishevelled hair and her crumpled clothes and went to the bathroom and started washing her face.

Saket went to the kitchen and kept water on the stove for tea. He laid the plates for breakfast on the table. He had thrown a kitchen towel over his shoulder like a bearer.

Deep Di felt somewhat light after washing the face. She smiled when she saw Saket with his shirt sleeves rolled up and wiping wet plates. She said angrily: "Why don't you sit there? Why have you barged in here? Leave these things —" She snatched the kitchen towel from him and took charge of the half-washed plates.

"Go and sit there. I'll bring the tea."

But would Saket take his seat so easily?

As Deep Di picked up the kettle, he went and kept the milk jug and the sugar bowl on the table.

"So many cups and spoons! Why have you brought a whole pile of crockery? Today I feel that we should drink tea out of the same cup! Deep Di, I don't know what's happened to me today…!"

Deep Di smiled to herself and gave him a gentle slap: "You've become very naughty!"

Deep Di kept the spoon on the plate mixing sugar in the tea cups. As she offered one of the cups towards Saket, he picked up a sweet and held it to Deep Di's lips: "Please have this!"

"I say… should I give you the sweet or you to me?"

"I… I'll give you…"

"Why?"

"How does the world know that it's not me but you have passed the examination? The entire credit for my passing is yours, isn't it?"

Deep Di held his hand with the sweet and turned it towards his own mouth.

"Eat, please!"

Saket opened his mouth and swallowed the sweet without protest.

Deep Di lifted a cup of tea and held it to his lips.

Then neither of them said anything.

After breakfast, Saket wiped his mouth with the end of Deep Di's saree as usual.

Deep Di didn't say anything — only gave him an angry look.

Just at that moment, there was a knock at the door which startled them. Deep Di herself rose and opened the door.

It was one of Deep Di's students. Her father had been transferred to Agra and she had come to see her before her departure.

"Will you do your B.A. from there only?"

"Yes, please."

"Is your elder sister also there?"

"Yes, please."

"Is your father being transferred to a higher post?"

"Yes!" said the girl as she left. "Didi, do come to Agra sometime."

"I'll definitely come sometime." She sighed and said: "It seems the last days will be spent only in Agra, where there is a lunatic asylum," and she laughed at her own words.

"It's not that, Didi," the girl smiled and delicately pressing the end of her saree in her mouth, walked away.

After the departure of the girl, Deep Di closed the door and turned back. She found Saket leaning on to balcony supporting himself on the parapet wall. Only the back of the receding girl could be seen — like a yellow spot.

"Arrey, what are you doing seated here?"

"I'm thinking something, Didi!" he said tenderly.

"What?"

"Just that I should build for Didi a dam higher than Everest!"

"Stop it!" Deep Di kept her palm over his lips.

"Do you know that girl, Deep Di?"

"Of course! She studies in my college."

"Do you really think that she came to see you?"

"Whom else?" Deep Di made a face. "Do you think she came to meet you?"

"Indeed! Indeed!" Saket laughed.

"She's the sister of that Khagen, you know, your friend! When I went to give her tuition, on the first day, 1 asked her to write an essay on the cow. The following day when I went to her, I found that instead of an essay on the cow, she had written an essay on me — a lengthy love letter! 'What's this?' I was about to ask her when her father came to the room for some work."

"If the essay is good, let me have it, Saket. It will be published in the journal of our ministry."

"It's not fit to be printed yet, Sir..."

"After the father was gone, I threw those sheets of paper on her head." Saket became silent.

Deep Di stared at his face. "I thought you were a decent, honourable man!"

"That's where you blundered, Deep Di! How is being honourable related to me in any case?"

They both laughed at the same time…

After about two months, the postman stopped at his door with a registered letter. Saket opened it and found that it was a call letter for an interview on the 17th at three o'clock in the afternoon.

Deep Di saw the letter and said: "You must get some new clothes."

"How do clothes help, Deep Di?" he said with an air of carelessness. "I intended taking with me that old coat of mine. It's lying with you, isn't it?"

"I've thrown it away long ago," Deep Di said…

Saket went for the interview. Mr. Badhwani, the Chairman of the Commission was highly impressed by him.

About a fortnight later, the successful candidates received their appointment letters. All of them went to the Central Office. But none of them was willing to go to Kashmir, Ladakh and Andaman and Nicobar. Hence, the office arranged a meeting to which the candidates were specially invited.

The elderly Director sat in his chair, repeatedly passing his hand over his jute-like grey hair. There was a lot of informal talk. He informed the candidates about how he had spent many valuable years of his life in the dense forests of Assam and the foothills of the Himalayas. A huge map of India hung on the wall behind him. He got up and with the help of the pointed end of his stick explained to them how he had passed those years in those places at a time, when modern facilities were not available. Then he explained many other things with the help of the map.

"Here, Pakistan has appropriated all this area by invading Kashmir under the cover of the Kabailies — the tribals." He moved the pointer over the map in a crooked line and said: "We have to build new bridges in these border areas and have a network of roads. We have become free after being under foreign domination for over a hundred years, and after making so many sacrifices. The responsibility of protecting these areas lies with young men like you, on your morale, your hard work, your courage."

He wiped his sweat with a handkerchief.

The end of the pointer now moved downwards: "These are the Andaman and Nicobar Islands." Then pointing out the Bay of Bengal he said: "Known by the notorious name of Black Waters, this area has to be rehabilitated. We have to build new roads in the dense forests there. Bengali refugees from East Pakistan have gone and settled there. We have to provide them with the basic amenities so that they can keep themselves alive."

Then moving the stick from Calcutta to Kanyakumari he said: "This is our sea coast, which is unsafe so long as the conditions of the Andaman and Nicobar Islands are not consolidated. The Andaman Islands are like our sea fort. We need roads there and new bridges and runways. We need new ports. It's quite possible that the climate of that place won't suit most of you. And there may be many other hardships. But we shall have to face such adversities in the interest of the nation. The future of this ancient land is in the hands of young people like you. The country needs your sacrifices."

Again he passed his hand on his grey hair. He wiped his perspiration and drank water from the glass kept in front of him.

"Well, how many candidates are willing to go to the Andaman Islands?"

All of them looked at each other.

"None of you is…" Before he finished his sentence, Saket was on his feet. Following his example, seven or eight more candidates stood up.

"That's enough. We require only five engineers in this batch and only three for Kashmir."

The Director had another special meeting with those candidates. He patted them on their back. He assured them that they would be granted special allowances for going to those places. And they would be given five increments in advance. They would be provided with all the facilities for boarding and lodging. Moreover, the government would bear their travel expenses over and above their medical expenses.

The Director was highly impressed by Saket's simplicity, spontaneous behaviour and boundless enthusiasm.

"You were the first person to register, isn't it?"

"I sent for your application again and read it. So, you've broken the university record, eh?"

Saket didn't say anything.

"What do your parents do?"

"Nothing, sir!"

"Something at least...."

"They are both deceased, Sir!"

"A steamer would be leaving from Calcutta in a fortnight's time."

Deep Di's gaze was fixed somewhere helplessly. She held in her right hand an unfolded white sheet of paper. She felt as though that paper was covered from top to bottom with the name of the Andamans. The grip of her fingers was so tight that it almost crushed the paper. Pressing her lower lip under her teeth she steadily gazed in front of her.

"Won't you say something?"

Deep Di really didn't say anything. She merely glanced at him once.

"There's something like duty too, isn't it?" Saket said as if to himself. He held on tightly to the railing with both his hands. Then resting his elbow on the railing he stared into the darkness. A steamer would leave within a fortnight from Calcutta.

He swirled back and asked: "Won't you say something?"

"What should I say?" Deep Di's voice choked.

"I've got the train reservation for the day after tomorrow. I shall be in Calcutta for a day. The steamer would be sailing on the fifteenth. I shall send you a wire before leaving."

There was no response from the other side — except the sound of the rustling of the paper in the dark and a deep sigh.

"Come there during your summer holidays…"

"…"

"Chhaya's eyes have to be treated. Please take her to a good doctor. I shall send the money."

"…."

He held the fluttering end of Deep Di's saree in his hand and started winding the extreme end around his finger.

"I shall have to be born again to repay my debt to you — you've done so much for me, Deep Di!" He rested his head on Deep's stooping shoulders…

A bird fluttered its wings and flew through the darkness.

Saket was seated on a broken cot. Inside the house, Roop had been boiling potatoes. Chhoti Ma was in her puja room. Anni was seated on a teapoy reading a children's book that Saket had brought for him just that day. Chhaya, seated in a corner, was stroking a cat.

The meal was ready after some time. Roop brought food for Saket on a metal plate. He was awakened from his thoughts as it were: "Arrey, you've already finished cooking! You've become an expert cook by now!"

Roop felt embarrassed to hear the praise. She kept the plate on the teapoy. As she turned to go to fetch water Saket called her.

"Come here!" he said, as she stopped hesitatingly. "Bring everything you've cooked here. Today we shall all eat together."

Roop brought dal and rotis. They started eating from the same plate.

"Doesn't mother take even fruits at night?"

"No!"

"Not even milk?"

"No!"

"Then without eating…" Saket became silent.

They continued eating in silence. Only the sound of their chewing the rotis could be heard.

"You better join school again, yes!" he said looking at Roop.

"After I've grown so big…!"

"Arrey, you think you're big, is it? In our days, girls of your age used to study in upper primary, whereas, you will get admission in the ninth class!"

"And if Anni studies hard, I shall send him lots and lots of presents — right?" he added.

Anni's cheeks were puffed up with the piece of roti stuffed in his mouth. He merely nodded his head.

"And Chhaya, when I come here on leave, you would recognize me when you see me from the distance of a mile, won't you?"

Chhaya groped for food on the plate.

"You've stuffed me with too much food today, Roop!" Saket said, and emptying the glass of water, kept it aside.

"You've eaten just two rotis?"

"Only two! I've eaten ten rotis, yes!" Saket laughed.

"What will you eat there, Bhaiya?" Roop asked.

Saket replied lightly, "Roots, fruits — whatever is available!"

Saket paced up and down in the courtyard. After walking for some time, he sat on the charpoy. Roop collected the used utensils.

"Father was jailed there, wasn't he?" Roop asked. Saket nodded in reply.

"Do send the photograph of the cell in which father was kept."

Their house was old-fashioned with very few amenities. Hence, Saket arranged for a new house for them. He had new clothes stitched for everybody before leaving. He told the grocer: "Give them anything they need. Don't worry about money — I shall send."

"Why are you spending so much money, Bhaiya?" Roop asked.

"Why are you bothered?" He gave her a gentle slap

He came back from the gate: "Finish packing my luggage, Roop. Doing it in a hurry would cause a lot of trouble…"

Deep Di was seated on the edge of the bed, lost in her own thoughts. She had spread a whitish cloth on her knees on which she had been doing embroidery. But every now and then, her hands stopped. His face was expressionless, like a stone. Then she woke up to consciousness for a moment. Her fingers got entangled in the silken threads.

It was still dark in the room. She had deliberately not switched on the light. She liked sitting in solitude in that semi-darkness.

Opening wide the half-open door, Saket entered without any formality, all soaked in the rain.

"Why it's so dark here today?" His hand groped for the switch on the wall. The sound of the clicking of the switch could be heard. The room got flooded with light.

He drew the chair and sat opposite her. Water dripped from his clothes but he was the least bothered.

He sat with one knee over the other, resting his elbows on them and putting all the weight of the head on his wrists.

"I was thinking — tomorrow at this time I would be seated in the Howrah Express... Small swinging coupe, and the shrieking engine!" he muttered looking at Deep Di.

Deep Di's eyes were lowered and her face was gloomy.

"Did you cook in the morning?"

Deep Di didn't reply.

"You will sustain yourself by going hungry like this, isn't it?" he said angrily.

"..."

Neither of them spoke for a while. "I haven't got clothes," Saket said, trying to break the icy silence. "A pair or two will suffice for the moment. I can manage."

Deep Di still didn't say anything. Saket snatched away the needle and thread from her hand. "I'm saying something to you, Deep Di!"

Deep Di raised her large tearful eyes to him. "Then go and buy. Saket, I really don't feel like going anywhere today."

"Why? I hope your health is all right?"

"Yes, I'm all right."

"Then what's the matter?"

"Nothing. You go without worrying and buy the clothes of your choice. Go now, otherwise, the market will close."

Saket stared at her in silence.

"Go, I tell you," Deep Di said in despair.

"Please go. I won't be able to go with you."

Saket went up to the door but came back. "Please Deep Di, come with me! Why are you unnecessarily pestering me?"

"Please go, Saket. I shall keep the food ready." She led him to the door. "You've become a big man now. How will you keep coming to eat Deep Di's dry rotis?"

Saket stared at her steadily. He went down the stairs. Deep Di still stood there staring at him.

Saket opened the iron gate and disappeared. Deep Di still remained standing there staring behind him.

Saket felt as though two tearful burning eyes were stuck to his back, and that those eyes followed him wherever he went.

Saket reached home quite late. He saw that his Mamaji had arrived from the village. He was crying after learning about Saket going to the Black Waters. He had not forgotten to bring with him a few close relatives to cry along with him.

He had hardly crossed the threshold and entered the room when his aged Mamaji came and clung to him, asking: "Why did you get such a harsh sentence?"

Saket sat on a tin in his wet clothes.

"I've not been sentenced, Mamaji, who does ever get a chance like this to serve the country?"

Mamaji said that his father too had served the country. What did he gain by discarding the prospering family and undergoing imprisonment in the Black Waters? Children had to knock from door to door. It was indeed because of the merit earned in the past life that a promising child was born to this house, otherwise…"

"Who knows if it is the merit of the past life or Father's own good deed, that is now bearing fruits?"

Saket tried to convince his aged Mamaji that he would be there for two or three years and then come back He said that Andaman Island was no longer inhabited by the convicts. There, too, the same kind of people lived as here. They were engaged in trade, and with some effort, that place could be transformed into a lovely tourist spot.

Mamaji simply nodded as though he had understood everything…

The railway compartment was overcrowded. Saket was seated near a window. Chhaya put her hand through the window groping to find Saket. Dada Babu was arranging the luggage on the upper berth. Saket leaned out of the window — he couldn't find Deep Di anywhere in that crowd.

Rattan's mother had kept for him a snack of parched grains to munch during the journey.

The green flag was waved. The guard blew the whistle. The wheels started moving slowly. Several hands rose and waved in the air at the same time. Anni ran with the train.

Saket brought his head down on the elbow resting on the window.

There was only the sound of the train in motion, of the shrieking train and the rattling iron wheels!

SIX

The climate of Calcutta seemed to be slightly different. A strange kind of sultriness, unbearable heat. And persistent torrential rains. Roop had kept a spare set of clothes to change during the journey. But Saket had been managing with the same old clothes. In fact, he was unconcerned about clothes as ever.

He came out of the bathroom and changed clothes. Roop said: "You've been hustling me since yesterday to pack your things, but what's there to pack?" Saket didn't remember what he had said in reply.

He had made a telephone inquiry just before going for his bath — the steamer was likely to sail for the Andamans on time. He quickly gathered his luggage. Paid his hotel bill. Cutting through the heavy rush of trams and cars, his taxi was speeding towards the Kidderpore docks.

The steamer had been anchored at the dock for a long time. The platform was overcrowded with the passengers bound for the Andamans. What a noise! And people running in all directions! Getting off the taxi, Saket stood for a while watching with astonishment the scene around him.

The window of the weather office was hidden behind human heads. It was not yet time for the low tide. Only when the tide began to recede would the anchor be lifted and the swaying ship would start floating.

Cabin No.24 had been reserved for Saket in advance. He put his luggage in the cabin and came on the deck. He walked up and down surveying the scene.

The majority of the passengers on the deck were Oriya and Bihari labourers. The passengers on the bank seemed to be from the middle class. There were also some traders. And some white- collared people engaged in various occupations.

Saket's eyes showed a strange kind of curiosity. The steamer looked like a demon. Strange people. Strange place! Strange atmosphere!

He checked the time every now and then. He felt that he had been given the wrong information — otherwise, the steamer should have been out in the sea already.

Suddenly, people's eyes turned towards the Hoogly. Gradually, the deep water began to rise. Like in the floods, its water was enclosing both its spreading banks. A number of small sailboats and the heavily loaded dinghies had started swaying relentlessly.

There was excitement all around. The rolling tidal waves carried the giant-sized swaying ships southward of the Hoogly.

The boats and innumerable steamers bound for Rangoon, Singapore, Vishakhapatnam, Sri Lanka etc. were on the alert, continuously blowing sirens to inform the passengers to keep themselves ready. The passengers were almost in a panic. Groups of seamen went briskly up and down on the boats loaded with jute. The boat laden with fish crouched hugging the shores.

The passengers rushed frantically towards the steamers. Carrying their luggage, they moved on blindly. Some of them were already on board, busy locating their places.

Gradually, the anchor was lifted. The steamer glided from the shore and moved towards midstream. On the shore, a few hands waved a few colourful scarves

Saket stood on the deck, looking around absent-mindedly.

Countless boats, cutting through the waves, glided in slow motion around his steamer. A kind of caravan was moving towards midstream. On the shore were innumerable sale-boats, that looked like a long row of ducks.

Far into the distance, smoke from the tall factory chimneys rose to the sky.

Seated on a wooden chair on the deck, Saket was lost in a world of his own! A eucalyptus tree… a small, ancient house… the road and on the road…

Now darkness had descended. The broad banks of the Hooghly and clusters of coconut trees still appeared to be moving in the opposite direction of the steamer. Saket looked at his watch.

More than six hours had passed.

"How far is the Ganga Sagar from here?" Saket asked. The gentleman seated next to him replied: "Another six to seven hours before you would be able to spot the Ganga Sagar!"

The voyage had not been particularly difficult so far with slow-moving waves and a smooth pace.

Saket returned to his cabin. He switched on the light and the fan. He had bought a few books in Calcutta and also a big map of India. He spread out the map on the table and started studying it.

Calcutta … Hooghly … Ganga Sagar — the Bay of Bengal and some spots — He tried to guess the distance of those spots.

The dinner gong was sounded at about eight o'clock. But he didn't go anywhere. He called for his dinner in the cabin and starting nibbling all by himself. He was not particularly accustomed to eating rice. He found the taste of the dinner a bit odd. He left half the food untouched. As he wiped his hands after a wash, he remembered how he used to wipe his mouth with Deep Di's washed saree! How he was delighted by Deep Di's angry words or her absolute silence!

He ordered coffee.

He didn't like the taste of the coffee either.

He came out on the deck. He found the clean open air pleasant. There were some other passengers who were seated on their chairs talking in the dark. Some of them had stretched their legs and were in the process of going to sleep, covering their faces with newspapers ... A couple at the far end was leaning on the railing with arms around each other's waists, pointing out the waves to each other.

Saket stood alone in a corner, still as a statue. He stared at the waves enveloped by the darkness, at the shore stretching afar, at the clusters of forest trees. Years ago, a steamer must have sailed along the same course!... Handcuffs on the wrists and heavy shackles on the feet... Two ember-like eyes peering through the sultry cell... How those eyes must have loved their land... what yearning for freedom and what delirious courage to march at the gravest risk to life!...

In the morning the bearer entered with bed-tea.

Rubbing his eyes, Saket looked out of the window — endless, fathomless water all around! Only water! No tree, no shore…!

"Are we nearing the Ganga Sagar?"

The bearer replied as he kept the cup on the small table: "We have left it far behind!"

Saket hung the map on the wall of the cabin. He examined the map and tried to imagine where the steamer would have reached at that point in time…

The sea had been smooth so far. Hence he didn't feel too much of sea-sickness.

He had a wash and went to the dining room for breakfast. He saw so many faces — but all flat. Not a single known face!

He sat at an unoccupied table. As was about to take his first sip of tea, he felt a heavy hand on his shoulder: "Hello, young man!"

He turned round to look. He felt he had seen that face somewhere...

"Do you recognize me?"

He frowned...

"Oh, yes! You're the Director, Sir!"

Both of them burst into loud laughter. Saket greeted him and pulled a chair. "Please have a seat!"

The Director sat without any formality.

"Where are you going, Sir?"

"The Andamans!"

Saket poured out tea for him. Didn't you go by plane?"

"Plane!" Director Badhwani laughed aloud. "Why by plane, dear, man? Had I gone by plane, how would 1 have got this chance of sitting and chatting with you?"

Saket smiled.

"Sugar...!"

"Only one spoon."

After stirring the tea with a spoon, Saket advanced the cup towards the Director.

"I don't think your other colleagues are taking this steamer, are they?"

"I didn't see them, sir!"

"Why were you in such a hurry? You had ample time before joining."

"How would I have got this opportunity of sitting and talking with you...!" Saket said. The Director burst into such a loud guffaw that the people sitting around them turned and looked.

After tea, both of them came on the deck.

Mr. Badhwani offered a cigarette to Saket which he politely declined. Saket drew a chair for him, but he didn't sit.

The two of them kept staring in silence at the boundless sea.

"You took the trouble of coming here…!"

Mr. Badhwani continued to stare at the waves rising high up to the sky.

"It's no trouble, young man. I consider it my good fortune," Mr. Badhwani said. "Whenever I find time for inspection, I make it a point to go. Hardly much time has passed since we became independent. However, I wish to see a few things get done while I'm still in charge. You can't imagine the condition of that place during my first visit there!"

A flock of marine birds suddenly appeared from a distance and came flying towards the steamer. The waves of the sea now rose higher and were more frightening. Seeing the indications of an impending storm, Saket insisted that they go in and sit in his cabin.

Without any hesitation, Mr. Badhwani went to his cabin.

He looked with curiosity at the map hung on the wall.

"Did you purchase this map in Calcutta?"

"Yes, Sir."

"I too had ordered a map yesterday. I don't consider a house without a map and a dictionary, a house of educated people," Mr. Badhwani laughed. Saket also joined in his laughter.

"How strange," Mr. Badhwani said, "That there's so much similarity between you and me! Just see, how we are travelling together! And we also cherish similar ideas?"

He turned the pages of the books that lay on the table. There was complete silence in the cabin.

There was a strong wind outside. Saket started collecting the papers that lay scattered.

"This is a very good thing you've done. It has been my experience of a lifetime that man cannot have a better friend in this world than books. What do you think?" He looked intently at Saket.

Mr. Badhwani's eyes were again fixed on the map.

"Sahib has sent for you," an orderly came and informed. Saket hesitated and got up, keeping the half-opened book on the table. Closing the cabin door, he followed the orderly.

He found Mr. Badhwani, dressed in a khadi kurta-pyjama, engrossed in the pile of papers scattered in front of him.

"Hello! You've come!" he looked at Saket with his usual natural smile.

Food had been laid on two small tables.

"Help us wash our hands, Amar!" Amar, the orderly, promptly poured water on his hands and then advanced towards him the towel hanging on his shoulder.

"Sit, don't just stand and stare."

"Sir..."

"Don't say, 'Sir'! Sit and relax. I don't like bureaucracy. What do you think — am I not right?"

Saket sat with much hesitation.

"How did you complete your studies!"

"By giving tuitions, Sir…"

They started eating. Stuffing a big morsel in his mouth, Mr. Badhwani asked: "Who all are there in your family?"

"Mother and four brothers and sisters."

"I think you said earlier that your mother had passed away!"

"Yes, Sir, my mother is dead. I have a stepmother. I consider her to be not only a mother but a lot more than a mother."

"Are your brothers and sisters her children?"

"Yes, Sir."

"Who supports them?" He asked after a pause.

"Well, Sir, I'm there to support them. And then..." he stopped midway.

"Arrey, you're not eating! My dear, you are eating so slowly — is that the way you should eat? At your age, I used to eat four times this quantity."

Saket as though shrank within.

"The one who can't eat can do nothing in the world. What sort of service can you render unless you're healthy? He insisted on serving more rice to Saket from the rice plate."

Saket protested, but the Director would not listen.

Mr. Badhwani ordered fruits after eating the fill. After nibbling a couple of pieces himself, he kept the whole plate in front of Saket.

"You'll get up only after finishing the whole plate..."

Lunch over Mr. Badhwani was back at his work. He was not at all conscious that Saket was around. Ultimately, Saket quietly walked away.

Mr. Badhwani came out in the evening. Standing on the deck, he watched the setting sun.

The sea was rough again. The waves dashed against the sky. Jet black clouds came surging up from all sides. Every now and then, lightning flashed on the Western horizon. Soon there was a slanting drizzle. Surrounded by the stormy sea, the steamer continuously shook like a dry leaf on the water.

By now, half the passengers were in the grip of sea-sickness. Saket felt heaviness in his head and nausea. He lay on the bed in his dark cabin, face downwards.

Suddenly the door opened and someone came in, with water dripping from his clothes. A hand groped for the electric switch, and instantly that small cabin was flooded with light. A heavy hand stroked Saket's head.

"I hope you haven't eaten anything in the evening?"

"No, sir…"

"It looks like you are falling sick again."

There was no response from Saket. Turning on the bed, he tried to sit up.

"Oh, no don't get up, dear man! Take this medicine for the time being. Soon, the doctor will be here."

SEVEN

The sea was now calm and the sky was clear. Saket felt weak, as though he had just recovered from a long illness.

Amar stood before him with a bottle of medicine.

"What is Sahib doing?"

"He is engaged in his work."

"Does he work during the night too? When I got up at four o'clock in the morning, I found the light on in his cabin."

"Sahib hasn't slept for the past three days. He just stretches on the easy chair and sleeps for half an hour or so," Amar said. "Sahib doesn't even remember to eat and drink."

Saket took the medicine and sat on the chair. His legs were paining after lying down the whole time. Amar had left in the meantime.

In the evening, Mr. Badhwani was sitting on a chair on the deck. Saket was sitting on the opposite chair. The news was being relayed on the transistor.

Both of them were silent. Now the transistor was silent too. The blast of moist air passing over the sea was very pleasant.

They had probably been discussing something earlier — that is, to a large extent, Mr. Badhwani did the talking. Saket had been quietly listening.

Closing his eyes, Mr. Badhwani shook off the ash from his cigarette and said: "One needs liquor in order to be able to live. If that liquor is associated with some mission or purpose, living becomes all the easier," he coughed and said: "Now just look at me. I haven't married. I've nobody of my own. Still, I don't feel I'm alone. I'm struggling for a 'very large family.' It has its own kind of pleasure isn't it?"

He looked at Saket.

A pair of birds flew past them with the speed of an arrow. A marine eagle was seated atop the pole for a long time. Who could say what it was waiting for?

Mr. Badhwani got up and, placing his hand on Saket's shoulder turned and entered his cabin with a deep sigh.

One could only see two backs moving side by side and then they vanished.

The seagulls were flying along with the steamer. The sky which was washed clean by the drizzle of the previous night now shone bright with the rays of the rising sun. Tiny clouds, like balls of cotton, looked very pretty. Far into the distance, land could be sighted. The sailors on the deck looked at it through their binoculars.

It was the fourth day. The Andaman Island was gradually drawing close.

Saket found the sky very pleasant.

Mr. Badhwani stood by his side. Pointing with his fingers towards the coconut trees, he was explaining something to Saket.

Amar had kept the luggage packed and ready.

The sailors expressed their happiness by waving their hands from afar. The steamer blew the siren and soon the anchor was thrown near a circular island called Chatham.

Hundreds of people were standing on the deck. Before Mr. Badhwani could come down, a whole crowd of engineers and overseers on deputation surrounded him very affectionately.

He walked down very carefully.

As usual, the Chatham Sawing Machine was still engaged in sawing wood. The island, barely one square furlong in area, appeared very lovely today. The coconut trees bent low over the water, half sinking into the water as it were.

"Have these trees also grown old like me or what?" Mr. Badhwani remarked with a smile and everybody burst out laughing. He mixed with all members of the staff and talked with them on intimate terms — he was absolutely informal.

Saket followed him everywhere.

They all reached Port Blaire after crossing the wooden bridge that joined the two islands.

A jeep carrying the guests along with their luggage turned towards the Heddo Guest House. After covering a distance of barely three miles, they came to a halt before a very impressive bungalow.

Dark green coconut trees spread far into the distance, the wilt rubber and areca trees and some very high bamboo bushes in some places. On three sides, a heaving blue sea and islands scattered as far as the eyes could see. Saket walked beyond the corridor and discovered a new world altogether.

The following day. He went with Mr. Badhwani to see the Cellular Jail where, during British rule, political prisoners used to be sentenced to rigorous life imprisonment…

Saket had taken some flowers with him.

He went on the second floor — his father would have spent his last days in one of the cells there and his bones must be lying scattered in some comer of that island!

Mr. Badhwani narrated the background of each of those cells and Saket followed him like his shadow…

In one place were engraved the names of those martyrs, who had gone for their final journey there. Saket read through those names — there was also his father's name among them — Martyr Dinamani Azad.

A shiver passed through Saket's body when he read that name. For a long time, he stood astounded and lost in himself. He did not realize where and when the flowers dropped from his hands.

Mr. Badhwani put his hand on his shoulder and led him out. For a long time, Saket didn't utter a single word.

Mr. Badhwani then heaved a sigh and said: "It's the sacrifices of these very people ... Every drop of their blood has made the history of India. These are the sacred places of India from which future generations will draw inspiration. The earth of this place, this arid land is more sacred than any place of pilgrimage…"

Mr. Badhwani narrated the history of the very cell, where his own father had been starved for twenty-seven days and tortured to death.

"My mother wasn't mad in her last days," Mr. Badhwani said. "My elder brother who was unable to bear the tortures at the hands of the British authorities, ultimately committed suicide. I don't know how I managed to keep myself alive. We don't know how many people made great sacrifices so that we shall be able to attain our present state of freedom."

Whenever possible, Mr. Badhwani took Saket with him when he went for an inspection, so that later on he wouldn't find the place unfamiliar and unknown.

Standing on the Hope Town Jetty, he pointed out, "This is the very place where Lord Mayo had been murdered."

Within a few days, he showed Saket Dundas Pine, Bamb Palate, Jangli Ghat, Pahad Ganj, Girara Chama — in fact, all the small towns along their route. In Rangat Dweep he could see Rampuri, Dashrathpuri and several other ancient cities.

On the very sixth day…

Mr. Badhwani had a programme to go to Madras via Nicobar.

Before boarding the steamer, he strolled on the jetty with the engineers. He explained to them: "According to the plans, certain jobs should be completed more or less within the stipulated period under any circumstances. Prosperity has to be brought to all those islands and that could be done only when there are roads and bridges. And jetties should also be built all over. It wasn't proper that the unfortunate refugees who had come all the way to settle there should be faced with more hardships. All hardships had to be mutually shared and born. The life of those hapless refugees has to be raised to our level. So long as there is even one poor person in the country deprived of food and clothes, we are not free in the real sense. Our freedom is incomplete!"

He boarded the steamer. Several hands waved in the air. In no time, the steamer disappeared on the horizon.

Saket experienced terrible loneliness — a strange void which was utterly unbearable. He dropped himself wearily on the chair and looking at the whirling ceiling fan, was lost in thought.

That small fan was rotating fast as if to cut itself instead of cutting through the air. The cigarette smoke got diffused before it could form into any shape. As he lay there, his eyelids started dropping and he closed his eye tight.

It was the thunderclap outside that woke him up. He lighted another cigarette and started walking aimlessly on the verandah. It had been raining cats and dogs since morning. Bubbles were rising in the waterlogged at the threshold. Blasts of strong wind swept away the downpour. The earth has turned into an ocean. He had no doubt heard that it rained heavily in those parts — but he hadn't imagined it would be raining so hard. He took out and examined the plans for roads and bridges. But he could not concentrate and so, he rolled them up and put them aside.

It was time to go to work.

He set out without waiting for the rains to stop, picking up his raincoat and umbrella. He went to the site where the construction had been started the previous day.

The labourers were getting drenched in the rain under the rubber trees. The moment they saw him, they were all on their feet.

The aged jawabdar saluted him and stood before him. He informed that according to the instruction, the rubble had already been spread.

It wasn't now raining with as much fury, but it still rained in big drops.

Saket walked ahead. He himself picked up a stone on the course of the roller and kept it at the edge of the road. The jawabdar walked behind him, followed by all the labourers.

Khat. . .khat.. some men started breaking stones with hammers. Others started cutting and removing the trees that had fallen on the roads. Further down, the work of spreading the rubble had also been started.

"Ha..ee..Lo...La....ee! Ha., ee... ho... ha., ha. . . Ha....ee...ho...o...!" The Oungi tribal labourers were dragging along a gigantic vehicle.

Somewhere at a distant place, the work of the Forest Department was being carried on. Some policemen who had gotten off the police boat were going northward for their patrolling. There were reports about their encounter with Jarwah tribals.

Saket had hardly been in that place for a week when he got a transfer to Nicobar where suddenly some new work had been started. In view of the requirements of the Navy, a new military port was being built. Some small islands had to be linked by bridges. And jetties had also to be built on both sides of the port. Large batches of labourers were being transported from the Andamans. The whole force of the A.P.W.D. was turned over to the Nicobar Island.

One day, the anchor of a very big steamer was lifted from Chatham Yet again Rose Island, Vaypar, Andaman and Chatham were left behind. The angry, foamy waves of the sea dashing against the rocks could no longer be seen.

There were also other passengers standing by Saket's side. The sailboats of fishermen, with their nets gathered, were returning to the shore. A flock of birds flew along with the steamer for a long distance, but suddenly it was out of sight. Far into the distance, a steamer turned westward.

Saket returned to his cabin. Some magazines had arrived via Calcutta. There was also a bundle of daily newspapers. One by one, he savoured the news items and went on keeping aside the papers after reading. Reserving the magazine for his night reading, he took out the blueprints prepared by the draughtsmen and got busy working on them.

The sea was calm that day.

EIGHT

Adjacent to the Nicobar Island was a small isle laden with coconut and areca trees. At the western end was a small settlement of the Nicobar tribals. Casting their nets in the sea, those tribals caught enough fish to fill their dinghies. Some fishermen had also started working as labourers in the past few years. Some people collected coconuts and areca nuts and sold them in the shops of Akuji in exchange for the things they needed.

Nearly a hundred and twenty-five Bihari and Oriya labourers had been brought there by steamboats. They were now busy building roads. Lately, some Bengali refugees also had started working as labourers.

There were no human settlements anywhere in the terrifying forests that spread far and wide. Of course, some work was being carried on by the Forest Department. The passing steamers loaded with construction wood could also be seen.

The Nicobari tribals, however, did inhabit the islands at the eastern end in large numbers. They had been there for centuries, living their carefree lives. Except for catching fish, they did nothing else worth mentioning.

Saket found it all very odd on his arrival. The nominal amenities available in the Andamans were missing there. For a few days, he continued commuting by his jeep for inspection, covering nearly forty miles a day. But later he found it to be a futile exercise and he set up his little tent right there. He felt that he no longer had any contact with the rest of the world.

After coming to that place, he had the satisfaction that the work was proceeding speedily. Once in a week or two, he visited the site where the port was coming up. He was able to see many people and hear many things.

Some men were busy sinking pillars in water to build the jetties on the seashore. Saket examined the plan and explained some points to the overseers. The overseer was getting the work done by the workers, who were constantly at work like machines.

Saket looked at his watch. "Arrey, you people haven't taken your lunch break today! It's going to be three o'clock!" he said with surprise.

The jawabdar standing before him said: "They'll go for lunch after finishing their work."

"No…no!" Let them have their lunch first and rest for an hour or two. The work can be started again after five o'clock.

The headman beat the stick on a metal plate and promptly all the labourers picked up their respective bundles. They sat under the shaded trees and started eating their meagre meals cooked the previous night.

Saket washed his hands and feet. One man laid food for him from a tiffin carrier on a small folding ebony table.

A child was playing on the sand. Saket lifted him and placed him on the chair opposite him. While having his own food, he kept giving small bits of biscuits to that child.

In that place, one always got rice to eat-rice, and nothing else. Saket was not particularly fond of rice. Whatever atta was received last time, Saket had distributed among the people.

He removed the bones from the fried fish and put a piece in his mouth as he stared lost in thought, at the waves.

"Sahib, here's your water, and…!"

Without listening or even looking that side, Saket just said. "No!"

The orderly put a little packet of powdered salt before the sahib, who often used to sprinkle salt on pieces of fried fish.

Saket turned round to look at him.

"I don't need anything else. And, yes, have you taken your lunch?"

"I shall have it after I have served you, Sahib!"

"No, no!" Saket shook his head as always. "You also sit down and eat. We'll all eat together!" He looked at the child and threw another biscuit at him. Both the cheeks of the child were puffed up. His mouth was full.

As Saket turned back to pick up the jug of water he noticed something like a bundle lying near the waves on the wet sand.

"Who is that?" Saket looked at the orderly.

"Must be some Nicobari," the orderly replied carelessly.

"Just go and see. In this heat…"

After drinking some water, Saket got back to looking for bones in the fish.

The orderly came back and informed: "It's some woman labourer, a Nicobari… She is weeping."

"Why? Why is she weeping?" Saket asked, removing the thorn-like bones from the fish.

"Sahib, she says that the jawabdar hasn't given her wages...!"

Saket was silent for a moment. Then, after some thought, he said: "Call the jawabdar!"

The orderly went and called the jawabdar.

"Why didn't she get her wages?"

"Sahib, she doesn't work properly. Because she doesn't work well, she doesn't get the wages."

"No," Saket looked up and said. "Go, give her the wages and persuade her to work well. Everyone around here is eating. It's not a pleasant sight to see someone sitting alone without food and crying."

"She deserves that Sahib!" said the jawabdar and went away.

Saket washed his hands. Wiping his lips with his handkerchief, he suddenly remembered something…

A strong wind was blowing. The flame of the hurricane lamp on the table opposite was flickering. It was almost past midnight. Saket was engaged in office work. His fingers struck the keys of the typewriter briskly The plans were spread out before him like banana leaves.

Replies to some official letters — some of them urgent and some that had to go by the next morning under any circumstances.

Saket finished the work and stretched his limbs. He had no idea what time it was. He lighted a cigarette and stretched his legs over the table. The cigarette pressed between his fingers got extinguished as he fell fast asleep in that same position.

The orderly, who brought his tea in the morning, was surprised to find his sahib sleeping in that position. The sun was already up and the hurricane lamp was still burning.

Before going to work, Saket took a long walk by the seaside. The Nicobaris were returning with their dinghies loaded with fish. He wondered how early they must be going to work that they were already returning after finishing their work for the day!...

One of the labourers had said to him yesterday: "Five dinghies were overturned in the storm day before yesterday. Nobody knows the fate of twenty-five fishermen!"

Saket thought: "If these people were given motorboats for fishing, how much bigger their catch would be and how much they would prosper!"

Returning to his tent, he called his subordinates. He gave due consideration to their difficulties. He called the jawabdars and explained to them how they should deal with the labourers and get the work done by them. He corresponded with the government departments and got the labourers' wages raised from the previous month. This time, too, he had the sealed tins of milk distributed for their children free of charge. He wrote to the central office for a mobile dispensary. A slightly educated jawabdar occasionally refreshed their knowledge of the alphabet at night. Lately, some tribals. too, had started taking an interest in studying.

The police motorboat had been patrolling the area almost every day. It was through these boats that he had been sending his mail.

One day, as he was about to leave for work, he noticed a few Nicobaris standing near the pathway. The jawabdar was talking to them in a threatening tone.

"What has happened so early in the morning?" He walked up to them with a smile.

"She doesn't work but asks for her wages..." the jawabdar replied, pointing at a crying girl. "The wood meant for the jetty ... there.... there...!" he waved his hand towards the sea, "There!"

"Thrown into the sea, is it?"

With an angry glare, he vigorously nodded his head several times — as if to confirm that fact.

"Who threw the wood?" Saket asked.

He pointed at the girl. Why? What happened? Why did you throw the wood in the sea?"

The girl kept quiet and stared blankly. "I'm asking you, why did you throw away the wood?" Saket repeated the question.

But the girl continued to stare as before — as though Saket had been talking not to her but to someone else.

"Tell me, why do you do such unwarranted things?" Saket moved a little closer to her and asked angrily.

"Tomorrow also she won't work but she will surely demand her wages," said the jawabdar.

It was probably the same girl yesterday — Saket remembered. The girl's dry hair was dishevelled. And her body was covered with tattered clothes.

"Speak up!" he said a little gently, "jawabdar, ask her, what's the matter?" Saket said turning to the jawabdar again.

Before the jawabdar could ask her anything, tears welled up in her fiery eyes. With a jerk, she turned away and started running towards the forest.

Saket called a Nicobari who had a smattering knowledge of Hindi and ordered the rest of them to get back to work.

"What happened?" he asked that man, walking along with him.

The Nicobari said: "The jawabdar doesn't give full wages. And if anyone protests, he beats him up with lathi and stones. Since the last month, that girl hasn't received even half her wages. Yesterday, he hit her head with a stone and pulled her hair…"

"Is the girl alone?"

"Her father drowned. Her mother…" He raised his finger and bent it like a bow to indicate that she was very old and infirm. And then, pointing out his eyes and ears he indicated that the old woman could neither see nor hear. Then he pointed at the stone under a tree and became silent. Then, after little thought, conveyed that the two had been hungry since the previous day.

"They haven't got anyone else?"

He merely shook his head in the negative.

During the day, Saket called the jawabdar during the off time.

"Has she come for work?"

The jawabdar shook his head and said: "She isn't working even today. The planks for the jetty had to be carried to the site, but she had started digging the road instead. She didn't take the instructions."

Saket remembered that the Nicobari had mentioned her head injury. Perhaps she was in no position to carry the wood.

"Sit down!"

The jawabdar sat down.

"Are you paying her full wages?" Saket asked hotly.

"She isn't working…" he stopped midway.

"If she is not working, then you're doing all the work, is it?" Saket was really angry. He ordered the overseer that he should be made to pay all the Nicobaris who had not been paid by him and he should be disgraced and sent back to the Andamans by the first steamer!

The overseer took the jawabdar with him and left.

The orderly laid the meal for Saket as usual. As he sat down to eat, he suddenly remembered something. He called the orderly.

"Listen, this Nicobari girl is hungry. Give her something to eat. And apply iodine on her head, otherwise, the wound will get septic."

The orderly just stood there. Probably he hadn't understood what he was told.

"Arrey," Saket clarified, "I mean that girl who had been crying yesterday."

Saket started picking the bones in the fish. His eyes were riveted on the waves yet again.

The meal was over in no time. He took out an inland letter from his bag and after writing just a few lines, folded it.

The overseer came from the camp, at night. He informed Saket that the jawabdar had paid off all the labourers and was crying. He had a large family and had been pleading that he shouldn't be sent to the Andamans. He said that a new jawabdar should be appointed in his place the next day. As for himself, he would be working as an ordinary labourer.

"Do other jawabdars also behave in the same way?" Saket was hinting at the tribal labourers.

"Not exactly, but..." The overseer was about to say something but Saket cut him short and said excitedly: "What do you mean? If there's such a complaint in the case of any labourer, you people will be held responsible. Your jobs will be in danger!"

After a brief pause, Saket resumed: "These people are like dumb animals. The project depends on the labour they put in. Should they be subjected to such unjust treatment? Even if we can't give them full justice, at least let us give them their full dues for their hard labour. What do you think — should they work for you on hungry stomachs?"

The overseer stood listening with a bowed head.

NINE

While walking. Deep Di suddenly paused and pondered.

She sat before the mirror for a long time — she had no idea, how long. Her dry hair spread out like carded cotton. One by one, she was plucking out strands of grey hair, and then staring at the silvery white hair held between her fingers. She got a feeling that she had aged quite a bit over the last few days.

During that long interval, she had received just three letters from Saket — a mere twelve lines. Perhaps she had been expecting something else — wanting something else — probably…it was as though someone had dragged her down as she was climbing up the stairs.

"May I come in?" someone stood at the half-open door. Deep Di was taken aback.

"Yes, yes!" she turned round and said: "Arrey, Roop! What brought you here?"

"There's been no letter from Bhaiya for a long time…" She took a few steps forward and stood before her and looked questioningly at Deep Di.

"I did receive one letter."

Roop asked eagerly: "What did he write?"

"Nothing…" Deep Di stopped short.

"Then did he by mistake send a blank envelope?" Roop said so innocently that Deep Di could not help laughing.

"He did write something…that everything was going fine…"

"That's all? Nothing else?"

Deep Di shook her head.

Neither of them said anything. Both remained silent.

"Do sit down, why are you standing?" Deep Di said, looking at Roop. "Have you shifted to the new house?"

"Yes, we have."

"What are you doing these days?"

"Bhaiya had told me before leaving that I should get admitted to the school. So, I've done that."

"Have you just got admitted or are you also studying something?"

"Of course, I'm studying," Roop replied and then became silent. Then she suddenly said: "Do you have Bhaiya's new address?"

Deep Di wrote down the address on a piece of paper.

"Are you able to manage the expenses?"

"Yes. Bhaiya sends the money every month."

"How is mother?"

"As she has always been," Roop said, after a little thought. "Last time Bhaiya sent a photograph of that jail in the Andamans where our father had spent his last days. Mother broke down looking at the photograph. Seeing her crying, my younger brother Anni also burst out crying. And when Anni and Mother started crying, my younger sister also couldn't contain herself and started crying. And then all of us were crying. 1 wrote to Bhaiya also that we all cried together," Roop said with childlike simplicity.

Deep Di gazed at her innocent figure.

"Is Chhaya able to see with her eyes?"

"No, now she can see even less than before," Roop replied maturely. "Bhaiya will arrange for the treatment on his return. Then everything will be fine."

After Roop's visit, Deep Di was again lost in herself. That black coat with torn sleeves which Saket often used to wear still hung on the peg… "Deep Di, won't you give me something to eat? ... Won't you say something, Deep Di? ... I'll build a bridge for you ... and a big airport at your threshold ... you're crying, DeepDi…"

"She smelt the cotton wool and threw it away," the orderly said. "These Nicobaris are superstitious. They worship spirits. The wound in her head has become septic, but she doesn't apply the medicine. It's such a big wound — so big!" and he indicated the depth of the wound by measuring the finger with his thumb.

Saket, without paying attention to him, went on gulping his tea. His body felt very sluggish after coming to this place. Perhaps it was the climate. He was confused. Salty sweat… Huge mosquitoes. Poisonous ants. Snakes with wide hoods were also a frequent sight. The Nicobaris were fairly sensible. Had they been like the Jarwahas of the Andamans, they would have faced extinction long ago.

Within a few months, Saket had visited many distant islands, in some of which the Christian Missionaries had been active. It all seemed to him like a dreamland something seen in sleep which could never be a reality…

The jetty would be ready in a day or two. It would then be possible to land on the shore even by steamer. Other islands and the main Nicobar Island had then to be linked by road by building a connecting bridge…

The senior engineer had come for a visit the day before yesterday. He remarked: "You've completed the work in less than half the time. It is a record performance so far."

Saket asked for one more cup of tea. He had started taking a lot of tea after coming here. That may be one reason for his low appetite.

In the evening, he sauntered towards the huts of the Bihari labourers. He saw some Nicobari fishermen and close by, the huts of the Nicobari labourers, nearly in shambles. People sat around a fire and seemed to be engaged in something like black magic…

In one corner of that settlement sat an old woman. Close to her was a girl. Some rags hung from a post. They had nothing of their own except the wide open sky and a tiny strip of land.

Saket sat on a rock, gazing at the waves surging towards the shore. That day, after a long time, the sailboats were in sight. He guessed they must be Akuji's boats. In exchange for areca and coconuts, those boats would bring some utility items for the tribals. He was amused by the simple nature of the Nicobaris. On the weighing scale, there were areca nuts on one side and salt on the other. Equal weight and equal joy on both sides.

Up front, some people were fishing in the sea. He lay flat on his back on a rock. A song was playing on the transistor kept nearby. Cool breeze, a blue open sky.

Then the transistor was silent. Saket remained stretched there, still like stone. He got up as the night descended. Hanging the transistor on the shoulder, he walked towards the shore, his feet sinking in the sand as he walked.

The same song was heard again from the cluster of the trees — sung exactly in the same way, and the same words — sung without the accompaniment of instruments — as though someone had been casually humming it.

He turned around and looked. The fishermen were returning home after gathering their catch of fish in their respective nets. He didn't realize when the song had stopped. It wasn't heard any more.

How strange were those people! He couldn't understand them. They worked hard all through the day and caught fish morning and evening. Beating their drums, they sang and danced around the fire throughout the night — when did they sleep?...

After dinner, he read for some time. After turning a few pages of the book he discovered in it a letter which had been stamped umpteen times. It had been re-directed from the Andamans. Only a few lines…

"It's you who have gone to the Andamans, but actually we at this end seem to have been condemned to that sentence… seated right at home… I don't expect much… just an occasional word from you! My eyes have started hurting, waiting for the postman…"

Saket left for work a little before time. There were a few Nicobaris standing by the roadside, laughing aloud.

He was very fascinated by their carefree life. How cheerful they could be despite their deprivation. He felt as though 'civilization' and 'happiness' were two separate entities.

He went closer — the same Nicobari girl stood in their midst, speaking fluent English.

He was astonished — the same news that he had heard the previous day while he was directing the labourers to do their work. "…This is All India Radio…"

As soon as she finished speaking, everybody applauded her and burst out laughing.

Following her example, a young boy jumped into their midst. He parroted a song exactly as it had been relayed by Radio Ceylon.

They all burst into an even louder laugh.

Saket smiled and walked away, keeping to the edge of the road so as not to disturb them in their entertainment.

That day, he constantly had one thought in his mind — if these people could be given education, how easily they would pick up things!

A grotesque-looking tribal boat moving away from the shore. Saket noted from the jetty that a girl with a dirty bundle by her side was sailing that boat.

Saket noticed that the naughty girl hadn't come that day. She hadn't come the previous day nor would she come the day after. He inquired from a tribal jawabdar. The jawabdar said that her mother had been possessed by spirits. Since she could not be cured here, the girl had taken her mother for exorcism to another island where their deity was supposed to reside.

That girl returned to work after a fortnight. Saket found her face shrivelled. She looked very sad as she busied herself with digging the earth mechanically.

The Nicobaris said that her mother would never get well. She would soon die. The deity was displeased with her…

One day, while walking along the road, Saket noticed somebody with a bleeding wound on the head... He turned back — it was the same Nicobari girl.

A doctor appointed for the Forest Department happened to pass that way. In the evening, Saket took him along to the tribal settlement. He found that girl eating raw fish.

The doctor examined her. The Nicobaris came out of their huts and crowded around, looking on with awe and wonder.

While leaving, the doctor took out some pills from his bag and gave them to her. When pressing her wound, he took out the Pus, the girl started shrieking. But under Saket's order, the tribals held her tight, not letting her run away.

The orderly came every morning and took the jawabdar with him, made the old woman take the pills and every third day, cleaned the wound and changed the bandage on the girl's head. The jawabdar stood there until the whole process was over.

Now the girl had started going to work as usual. The old woman's health also showed improvement.

Saket had obtained some necessary first aid equipment for use whenever necessary.

The rains had somewhat subsided. Hence everybody had been frantically trying to complete building that stretch of road at the earliest so that it would be convenient to start the construction work on the island.

Saket was required to go to Nankari for office work. He had planned to come back in about a week's time. But on reaching there, he found the situation such that it took him exactly a fortnight to get back.

There was some respite from the loneliness he had been experiencing all along. In spite of being fatigued, he found himself very fresh. Some of the engineers known to him had come to work there just last month. Kashyap from Kanpur … Chandrakar Sood also turned out to be an acquaintance…

Saket made prompt enquiries about the progress of the work as soon as he returned. He was happy that all the work was carried out properly even during his absence…

While he was having his morning tea, the orderly informed him that the old woman had died during the storm two days earlier. After cremating her, the girl had gone away to some island to her relatives and the jawabdar had struck off her name from the list of the labourers.

Saket gazed steadily in front. The tea-cup remained in his hand and the cigarette continued to smoulder, unattended.

The orderly went away.

He awoke from his stupor after a little while. He did not drink tea from the cup again. He just dressed up and went to work.

"The deity had already said that the woman won't live…" the jawabdar said.

The Nicobaris said: "The girl has no close relatives. Of course, there are some distant relatives who…!"

The work began every day as usual and came to an end. Saket would return to his camp and lie listlessly on his bed.

When he felt bored lying in the room, he went out and took his solitary walk on the seashore.

The coconut trees. The chorus of the Nicobaris singing around the fire. The broken moon occasionally shone through the clouds. The sea was calm. There was only a steamboat heading somewhere.

He was seated on the sand. The waves reached the wet sand near his feet, but it seemed Saket was oblivious to it.

It had been raining continuously over the last three days. After coming here, Saket had never seen such depressing rains. The labourers had kept indoors in their huts. The work was absolutely at a standstill.

His tent had been pitted at home height. Hence, the rainwater, instead of collecting there, flowed down the slope. There were sounds of the coconut trees crashing somewhere. Saket wasn't aware of anything except the darkness and the splashing rain.

He couldn't say what time of the night it was. While reading, Saket's eyes started drooping. The curtain was drawn back. With the strong breeze, the spray of rainwater came into the room. The hurricane lamp was burning.

Suddenly, he heard someone's subdued crying and sobbing. He opened his eyes and closed them again — he thought it must be an illusion.

A little later there was the sound of somebody dashing against the tarpaulin of the tent.

Again he opened his eyes and then closed them.

Then the sobbing was heard very clearly. Somebody's back was pressed against the tarpaulin wall of the tent and there was a slight inward depression on the tarpaulin.

He picked up his torch and went out, getting drenched in the rain.

He saw something like a tightly tied bundle lying there.

He went closer and asked: "Who is there?"

The bundle, which was soaked in rain, moved and two innocent eyes peered through black tresses.

"You!"

She didn't say anything. She just stared at him, trembling with fear.

"Why are you sitting here?"

She was silent.

"Come, come inside. There's going to be a storm again…" There was no response from her. She simply started crying, hiding her face between her knees.

Saket, getting drenched in the rain, kept gazing at her. Then, without a word, he held her arm and led her inside.

She had something wrapped in a rag under her armpit. Very carefully, she hid it between her knees.

Saket took out a bed sheet and put it around her. She sat on the floor right near the entrance. She hesitated to move further inside.

"From where have you come at this time of the night?"

She was silent, her eyes drooping.

"Is your mother dead?"

"..."

"Go and rest on that wooden plank down there. You can go to your Nicobari settlement in the morning."

"..."

Saket recalled that the Nicobari labourers had shifted settlements. Perhaps she had lost her way.

After Saket's persistent insistence, she got up, shrinking with fear and went and sat on one side.

She was still holding that bundle under her arms. "What's in that bundle?"

She opened the bundle. There were some bones in it.

"Your mother..."

She nodded her head.

Both were silent.

The cigarette held between Saket's fingers was burning.

"You go to sleep."

"..."

He opened the book and tried to read, but couldn't concentrate. He leaned comfortably on the chair and stretched his feet on the table. The book lay on his face upside down.

Then he didn't know when his eyes opened. He found the hurricane lantern still burning. She was standing near the entrance leaning against a pillar. She was crying.

Saket got up in confusion. He went very close to her and said: "Why don't you go to sleep? Go and rest."

She continued giving him a fixed gaze and then burst into bitter tears.

Saket stroked her wet hair.

"Would things be solved by crying like this?... Go to sleep."

She silently went to a corner and sat there hiding her face between her knees.

The rain hadn't yet stopped. She had probably gone to sleep. Now Saket stood leaning against the pillar where she had been standing earlier. He was staring outside fixedly-heaven only knew looking at what!

Morning…

He did not know when she went away. Saket felt it was all a dream. His head was heavy for want of proper sleep. Hence he wasn't able to go anywhere that morning.

She had been coming for work on other days. Her face had changed considerably during the past few days. She was looking very weak. Nor did she have her former playfulness...

In the evening, all the labourers had gone back to their respective abodes. Saket saw that she was still seated there — there was still that black, solitary spot on the white sand.

Then she was not seen for the next three or four days. Maybe she had gone away to some island where fishermen lived.

"Did she take her wages before going?" Saket asked.

The jawabdar shook his head: "No."

TEN

The road construction would be over that very month. Then would follow the next phase of the construction. The survey of the new site had already been completed. Saket visited far-off places with the overseers, carrying the measuring-tape and binoculars.

Lately, Saket was getting so fatigued by evening that he was in no position to go anywhere. His eyes closed in sleep the moment he stretched on his bed…

On that day, after a prolonged absence, the full moon appeared in the sky. Again there would be high tide in the sea. Saket enjoyed very much watching the waves dashing and shattering on the rocks.

He could not stop himself that day. Lost in thought, he kept walking, his feet sinking into the wet cold sand…

There were clothes on her body, just in name — torn and tattered rags. By her side was a wet net containing many small fish. She was seated, folding up her knees, on a pile of dry leaves. Her face was crestfallen. Even a passing look at her figure aroused fear. Dry hair spread over her shoulders.

"Where had you been all these days?"

She continued to stare at him.

"Why didn't you come to work?"

"...."

"Why didn't you take your wages?"

"..."

He seemed to have run out of questions. They kept staring at each other.

"Get up!..." he said in an authoritative voice.

"Why aren't you getting up?" Saket got really furious.

She got up like an ignorant, obedient little girl.

"Come on!"

She followed him.

Everyone was asleep. A yellow, sickly light spread inside Saket's tent. The globe of the hurricane lantern looked dim. In spite of dire poverty, there were no thefts in that place. Hence all things lay scattered inside as well as outside the tent. The orderly was not to come that day. He had a relative in the camp of the Forest Department. He would spend the night there.

"Keep the net outside." She kept the net on a heap of stones and then stood there.

"Why are you standing there? Sit inside," he said indicating a chair. Terrified, she tried to sit at the edge of the chair, casting panic-stricken glances all around.

"Why don't you sit comfortably?"

Looking down, she sat on the chair cross-legged. Her mud-stained feet soiled the washed cushion of the chair. She gave Saket a frightened look when he frowned and quickly getting up, sat on the floor. Though angry, Saket could not help laughing.

"Uncouth girl!" he muttered.

There was water in a bucket. Saket made her wash her hands and feet and kept a mirror in front of her. With astonishment, she saw her reflection in the mirror and then bashfully lowered her eyes.

"Did you eat anything?"

She pointed out the fish.

Saket kept in front of her the food that had been brought for him. She swallowed that food without saying anything. Who could say how many days had it been that she had gone without food?

Saket sauntered outside, with a cigarette pressed between his lips.

He returned after a long time. He saw that she had already finished eating the food. She sat staring steadily outside. What she had been thinking, was anyone's guess.

"What are you thinking sitting over there? There's water in that jug. Wash your hands," he said, pointing at the jug nearby. She understood what he meant.

She came in after washing her hands. Saket observed her — the bones of her body were jutting out. Crusts had formed on her drooping lips. She wasn't even able to hold the jug properly.

"Had you been ill?"

Probably she didn't understand what he had asked. She gave him a puzzled look.

He took his own bedding outside, where a portable cot was kept.

"You sleep inside," Saket said and came out without looking at her. He had left a sheet inside for her.

There was darkness all around. Everyone had gone to sleep. The sky was now absolutely clear. Somewhere, far in the distance, crickets were chirping. The group dance of the fishermen was long over. Saket was aimlessly gazing at the sky, unaware of the burning cigarette.

In the morning, Saket woke up early. No tea would be served that day. So, he came inside to make his own tea. And he saw that the bedding had been rolled up on one side, and she was lying without covering herself. She was still snoring! She had kept the net and the fish near her head — covered with the cushion of the chair!

Saket lighted the stove and made tea. When he woke her up, she sat up with a jerk in confusion and rubbing her eyes, looked around her.

"Will you have tea?"

She stared at his face, wondering what he had been saying.

Saket picked up his cup and took it to his lips. He said: "What are you staring at? Drink!"

She also picked up a cup exactly like how Saket had done and took it to her lips as he had done. Saket found there wasn't enough sugar in his tea. Hence, he took a spoonful from the sugar pot and started mixing it. Following him, she also took a spoon of sugar and mixed it in her cup.

When Saket kept his cup on the floor, she also put down her cup in the same way. When Saket put his cup to his lips, she also did the same.

Saket observed all that very carefully. He could not stop himself from laughing. In response to his laughter which was like a gushing fountain, she also burst into unrestrained laughter. The gleam of her white teeth fascinated Saket.

She had gone really very weak. She wasn't able to lift the stones. She couldn't carry the wood. She couldn't dig the road. Her hands shook while breaking the rubble. Her perspiring face turned red.

Saket had given her light work to do. She cleaned his utensils. She swept his house. At times she brought water for the labourers.

The jawabdar took literacy classes for the tribal Nicobaris at night. She too sat with them and learnt to read and write. She had learnt the alphabets now and was able to count up to ten…

The Nicobari labourers were sitting around the fire. They had made a blackboard by joining pieces of black planks. Saket drew on it the map of India. He pointed out some small islands in the Bay of Bengal.

"What is this?" Saket asked pointing the end of a stick towards the map.

"Bharat!" replied all of them at the same time.

"Whose country is it?"

"Ours."

"What's the total population?"

"Fifty crores."

How quickly they could grasp all the details!

"Our country is very big," he said, opening his arms very wide. "See here — this is Kanyakumari! This is Kamrup! This is Kutch! On the top in the North is Kashmir…! Delhi is the capital of our country… This is the Andaman Island.... here is Port Blair. And this tiny dot — it's called Nicobar. Now did you see in which part of the country we are!"

They were all wonderstruck — how could they live in such a small place?

"And look don't step too hard on the land, otherwise we would all sink into the sea!" They all laughed at Saket's remark.

They enjoyed his talk as though it were a magic story.

Towards the end, with a view to testing them, Saket asked an old man: "What's your name?"

"Nekura."

"In which country do you live?"

"Bharat Des." (Bharat Desh)

"What's your mother's name?"

He thought for a while. Wrinkles appeared on his aged forehead. Then something suddenly flashed in his mind and he said: "Bharat Mata…!"

They all burst into laughter.

The old man got nervous seeing them laugh.

"Very well. What's your father's name?'

This time he replied spontaneously: "Mahatma Gandi!" (Mahatma Gandhi)

They burst into hysteric laughter.

She had collected a whole pile of coconuts. One whole corner of the tent was covered with coconuts. It caused great inconvenience to Saket. There was no living space left for him. One day, he asked her angrily: "What's this you have done?"

She stared at him like an innocent child.

"You could have kept these outside under a tree — all this muck!"

"…"

"What will you do with them?"

"I'll give to Akuji…"

"Then…?"

She pointed at her tattered clothes, "In exchange for these…!"

Saket broke into laughter: "I see, that's the thing!"

He went away to work. He thought — "What's all this, after all! This poverty! These poverty-stricken people!"

She tidied up the room. She cleaned the floor as it had become dirty. All sorts of weeds had grown around the tent. She cleaned the whole place and plastered it with cow dung. She planted wild, flowers. The land, now neat and tidy, gave out a fragrance.

On a tall teak tree in front, she had hung on the highest branch an earthen pot tied with a red cloth. She said: "Now the ghosts and the spirits can't cast an angry spell here. Nor would any untoward thing ever happen here."

In Saket's absence, she gazed at her face in his mirror now and again. She would hold the mirror at various angles. She made all sorts of faces and looking at her own reflection in the mirror, laughed like a mad person.

She turned the pages of Saket's bulky books. Like other Nicobaris, she too had a remarkable memory. She had learnt a lot during the past few days. Hence, while doing all those household chores, she also read every day, and whatever she had learnt, she passed on to the tribals.

She had broken one by one, all the crockery and porcelain utensils. One day, while cleaning the hurricane lantern, she dropped the chimney. She covered it on one side with paper that had darkened with the soot…

Observing other people, she had picked up quite a bit of knowledge about first aid. When alone, she often hummed the songs that were relayed on the radio. And sometimes, while singing her folksongs, she started crying, and her eyes turned red like the kalawa flower.....

Saket had gone to Port Blair on office work. When he came back, he brought from there two sarees and some books for the primary classes. She finished with these books in just a few days. She also learnt quite a bit of writing. When she wore a coloured saree, her feet moved as if she were dancing. Tucking the fragrant, multicoloured flowers in her hair, she looked at her reflection in the mirror and stood wonderstruck.

"Oh, what's your name? I keep forgetting!" Saket often asked and she stared at him wondering how he couldn't remember such a simple thing!

Then she said very calmly: "Nono…o!"

"Nono!" Saket would repeat, as though he had heard that name for the first time.

He laughed: "Not Nono, say 'yes, yes'," he said: "I shall call you Nina, yes!" And seeing him, she too laughed.

Quite often, Saket was required to keep awake and work all through the night. She would wake up every now and then and give him tea. When he went to work in the morning, she arranged his scattered papers.

She would pick up a purple flower from somewhere every day and leave it under his pillow.

If Saket got furious and asked: "What's this?" She said very seriously "There's a belief amongst our people that we get nice dreams because of this."

Saket tried to decipher something on her face. Then, after some thought, he said: "I don't get dreams at all!"

"You don't get dreams !" She said moving her head in astonishment. "Don't you ever get dreams?"

"I do get some dreams ..."

Saket got back to his work and she would just stand there staring at him, leaning against the pillar. Then she moved a little closer, still closer, and muttered seriously: "I hope you don't see a witch?'

Saket continued working as though he had been listening. After a while when she repeated her question, Saket looked up and said: "What are you saying?"

"I hope you don't see a witch in your dreams?"

"Oh, yes," he nodded his head: "I do see! Big, long teeth.... big eyes! Fire coming from her mouth!"

She came still closer. "Really, do you see her?'

"Of course, I see her. I really do "

"Then, aren't you afraid?"

"I'm afraid."

"You're afraid!" she repeated with surprise.

Saket looked at her with an ape-like expression on his face and then got back to his work.

The next day, When he was arranging his bed, he discovered that she had hidden a bone tied in a tiny packet of ash under his pillow.

"What's this?"

"That will keep the witch away."

"Do your work if your health is good!" the jawabdar told her. "The Sahib has said… If you do another kind of work, you get different wages!"

The next day onwards, she started going to work as before. She lifted the stones. She carried the soil. She worked the whole day. At night she taught the Nicobaris reading and writing…

When Saket was on the point of putting off the light after finishing his work at about two o'clock at night, he found her standing with a cop of tea. Without a word, she held out the cup towards him.

She went up to the door and hesitated. She turned back and came close to him: "Did you see the witch again?"

Saket stared at her. He said nothing and only shook his head, "No…"

She ran out and kept on running and disappeared in the dense forest. Far into the distance, a fire burnt where the tribal labourers lived.

ELEVEN

Saket had not been keeping well ever since he returned from his tour. He had no appetite. His limbs were tired the whole time. He often got a fever during the night.

The burden of work was also continuously increasing. There were orders to complete the work in a very short time. He had not had a moment's rest in the past fifteen days. He could hardly say which were all the islands he had visited in the survey boat.

He did take some pills but they didn't give him any relief. He had sent a message to the head office through the police boat that the doctor had not yet arrived…

Everyone had gone to sleep. Saket had his charpoy spread outside. On the teapoy at his head side burnt a hurricane lantern. There were some bottles and papers near the lantern. There was also a half-opened letter from Deep Di.

The chowkidar had gone to sleep after giving him medicine.

Far off somewhere, The Nicobaris could be heard singing to the accompaniment of music.

Saket's head was very hot. He could not bear the heat of his fever. His parted lips had dried. He was breathing fast like a bellow. The water jug by his side had long become empty!

He heard a soft sound. A shadow came closer and stopped hesitantly.

"Who's that!"

"It's me…"

"You! What are you doing here?"

She remained silent.

"The orderly is on leave. Wake up the chowkidar…and you go to your camp and sleep…"

She stood there in the same position.

"Why don't you go and sleep?" he groaned and said in a slightly raised voice.

She still remained silent.

"I'm telling you to go and sleep!" he said in a slightly raised voice.

She still remained silent.

"I'm telling you to go and sleep!" he said, breathing heavily.

She stood there still like stone. Instead of going away, she moved closer, still closer. She sat on the floor near his feet and rested her head on the frame of the charpoy…

There were no signs of his recovery in that place. The doctor came and wrote the report that his treatment was not possible there.

One day, a special petrol boat came and took away Saket.

There were no good medical facilities in the missionary hospital. There was no provision for medicines and no good doctors were available. Hence, Saket was being taken to the Government hospital at Port Blair.

Saket showed slight improvement after about a month's treatment. He was able to move about a little. After spending another three weeks, he boarded a steamer to go back to Nicobar…

When Saket reached his camp, he saw all tribal workers and others including the employees of the Forest Department, rushing to meet him. Only Nina was missing…

In the evening, Saket was alone. Seated on a chair outside, he was lost in some thought. In those moments of loneliness, the image that suddenly emerged before him was that of Deep Di! Her smiling face, weeping face! What all he hadn't been thinking! In her last letter, she hadn't written anything—she had sent only a blank paper…!

The doctors had advised Saket to avoid visitors and take complete rest.

He returned to the tent when it started becoming dark. He went through his papers. He read the letters he had received from home. When he felt heaviness in his head, he rested his head on the cushion and closed his eyes.

A long time passed. He didn't know when his eyes opened. He saw the flickering light of the lamp and Nina standing like a statue. They kept gazing at each other without blinking their eyes…

"Come here!"

She took a couple of steps forward and came closer.

"Sit down!"

She sat down.

Saket looked at her withered face— as though she hadn't eaten anything for several months…as though she hadn't slept for many months and had passed one whole age without a wink of sleep!

"Won't you say something?"

She kept silent.

"Do you get food to eat?"

She nodded her head.

"Do you go to work?"

She nodded her head.

"Do you get your wages?"

She started digging the earth with her toes.

"You've gone so lean…!" he passed his tongue over his crusted lips. "So lean that one can't even recognize you!"

He looked up at her — two big dark eyes brimming with tears…

She untied the laces of his shoes. She removed his socks. She gathered his things that lay scattered all over and arranged them neatly. She combed his dry hair. While returning to her own camp, she lingered at the door…

He was in a very strange mood! His mind was sad for no reason. He didn't like being at his camp the whole time. But he had no strength to walk far. Walking leisurely, he drifted towards the tribal settlement.

And he found Nina drawing a map on the blackboard with chalk. She was saying: "This is the map of Nicobar!"

He walked ahead, keeping count of the coconut trees. In front of him was the small settlement of the Nicobari fishermen. Nets were kept hanging in front of their houses. The smell of fish filled the air.

Terrifying masks of ghosts hung on the outer walls of some of the huts. Those masks were used for appeasing their deities or during their nocturnal group dances…

He found the seashore extending very far that day. Some boats were turning towards the fishermen's settlement. He sat on the chair. The moon, round like a platter, was coming up. There was a high tide in the sea, like a deluge. The sea which looked like molten mercury, was trying to leap to the skies as it were. The waves dashed down on the rocks in a frenzy. He got up from the sand and sat on a rock.

He stared unwinking at the endless, boundless mass of water. When his eyes got tired, he looked down and then stretched languidly on the rock.

He had no idea how much time had passed.

Closing his eyes, he was as though seeing a dream — he felt something like a warm touch of delicate fingers. He felt as if someone had combed his hair with fingers as if someone had taken his aching head on the lap... had held his face between two palms. The touch of those fingers was very pleasant — it was as though a wave of sweet water had washed the entire rock! He experienced someone's warm breath very close to himself, and a touch of warm lips on his forehead- as though someone had kept burning coals there!

He wanted to turn on his side but couldn't do it. He wanted to open his eyes but couldn't. He wanted to speak, but couldn't utter a word...

The fingers knocking on the typewriter came to a stop. He raised his head and saw that she had kept both her hands on the machine.

"Tehh, tehh! What are you doing...?" When he tried to remove her hands she pressed the machine all the more.

"Will you let me work or....." he stared at her face. She gave him a naughty look in turn.

"Just a little..."

"No!"

"Why?"

"Doctor said, 'No!'" Saket laughed at her words.

With an angry gesture, she lifted the machine and kept it on another table.

Neither of them said anything for some time. They looked at each other in silence. Saket picked up a magazine to read, but she grabbed the magazine and flung it far with such force that its pages got torn. Saket got up and gathered the torn pages — "An ill-bred girl!"

She picked up the timepiece from the table and held it close to her ear. Then turning the face of the timepiece towards Saket she said: "Doctor..."

She blew off the glittering light of the lamp and laughing aloud, ran towards her camp where the chorus of the fishermen rung the air....

She carried the earth as usual. She broke the stones. Occasionally, she took literacy classes for the Nicobaris. She flung her net into the sea and collected a large haul of fish. She tidied up Saket's room. She kept humming and laughing.

"You're always busy doing things. Don't you get tired?" She laughed if Saket asked her sometimes.

Saket was astonished to see the way that girl had changed in just a few months. She had imbibed all the qualities that were found in any cultured and highly civilized society. She didn't give the impression that she was a tribal at one time. She wore clean clothes and kept them neatly arranged. She combed her hair daily. Her Ajanta-type hairstyles decorated with all kinds of flowers fascinated Saket very much. The rows of her pearl¬like teeth started gleaning after she rubbed her teeth with coal.

Saket was surprised when Nina talked in a very gentle and civilized manner. Sometimes, when he heard her singing and humming alone, he felt as though he were in a dream. Never before had he heard a voice so sweet and so melodious.

The bridge linking the Island with Nicobar was ready. And the five-mile road around the Island was made fit for driving jeeps... The same kind of construction was going on in other parts of the Island as well. Not much work could be carried on there because of heavy rains. Despite that Saket had established a record in the field.

It was possible to do some work in the area. A large number of small roads had to be built. The whole arid land would become rich if tubewells were sunk. Residential quarters for the naval force had still to be built. Traffic would become easier after building roads at the western end of the port. The place was of military importance in particular. Hence, the government wanted to start some secret construction work pertaining to naval bases.

Senior and chief engineers were highly impressed by Saket's work. He had worked under adverse and very hard circumstances with determination, efficiency and boundless enthusiasm which they all greatly admired.

With the climate and water being harmful, no engineer volunteered to come to that place. Even if he came by force of circumstances, he didn't stay there for long. But Saket had never complained. With the clearing of dense forests, the chances of getting malaria were automatically reduced.

The Senior Engineer frequently came for visits. This time, despite Saket's protests, the Senior Engineer had recommended his transfer. He was greatly worried about his steadily deteriorating health.

Saket felt that he would be leaving that place very soon. He had a special place in his heart for the people with whom he had lived all that time. As a result of his efforts, schemes for their reform were being implemented there too. If education could be spread among those poor and deprived people, they would breathe a fresh life…

"What are you making?"

"A map," she said carelessly without looking at him. "What map?"

"Map of India…"

He saw that she had drawn that map very well — as beautiful as a printed map — every line had come alive so to say!

"Show me Calcutta on this map." She put a dot in it with a pencil.

"Delhi!"

She put another dot.

"Do you know I'll be going back to Delhi? I'll be getting the Orders soon."

"Unh," she looked in front of her. "Leaving this place...?"

"Yes," he said, moving his head.

"I'll go with you…!" she insisted like a child.

"No!"

Saket's face grew suddenly grim.

"No, I'll go with you," she repeated, shaking her head.

"No!"

Suddenly she was on the point of tears. She put down everything—the map, the paper, the pencil…"No!" she repeated. Saket laughed at her simple-heartedness.

Now Saket remained somewhat out of sorts. He didn't speak to anyone. He buried himself in work. Nina couldn't understand why Saket had become so irritable. Why did he lose his temper over anything and everything?

"Won't you talk to me?" she asked.

"No!"

"Did I make any mistake?"

"No!"

"Then why…?" she came closer to him and stood hesitating.

Saket was silent.

She went still closer and stood there undecided. She raised her face and looked at him. "No, never!"

Saket moved backwards and holding a branch firmly, stood before her like a question mark.

Her hair was flying in the air. She stood there trembling, suppressing within her clenched fist the storm rising within her.

Saket didn't know why she too had been keeping away from him. Saket thought that it would be good if she too could be a little distant from him. It was quite likely that she would be able to absorb herself in her familiar life once again…

There was a tiny shed very close to the tribal settlement. On his return one night, he found her seated alone boiling the fish. Dry banana leaves lay scattered around. She was lost, deep in thought, burying her head between her knees…

The scope of work had vastly expanded. In all probability, some new overseers and engineers would be appointed. It was very difficult for Saket to attend to all the work by himself.

Saket had no idea when, during his absence, Nina came to his room, swept and tidied up the place. As far as possible, she avoided coming face-to-face with Saket.

The jawabdar had informed everyone that Saket would be leaving and a new Sahib would come in his place.

Saket sent for Nina, but she didn't come. One day, however, he ran into her. It was raining cats and dogs. Both of them were thoroughly drenched.

"Where are you going in this rain — do you want to die?"

She stood there with her eyes fixed on the ground, bowing her head and soaking in the rain. When it started raining more furiously, Saket moved from that place and stood under a shaded rubber tree. She too followed him and stood on the other side.

Water dripped from the leaves of the tree. Both of them were silent.

"You're drenched all over," Saket touched her wet clothes, as though wanting to make sure how much she was drenched.

She was wet from head to foot — as if she had just come out of a pond!

"Why didn't you cover your head?" he touched her wet tresses with the tips of his fingers. Nina shrank still further and her size reduced as it were.

"You aren't combing your hair any more! You don't even dress properly!"

He stroked her wet hair. Then he held her sad face between his palms and raised it. "You've become dumb now, isn't it? You can't speak! You can't laugh! Look at your face!"

He gazed steadily at her — her large eyes were blurred. She closed her eyes very tight. Her diy lips trembled.

"You're very strange!" Saket muttered. "You've gone back to the same old state— the same appearance. You've grown so big, but your nature hasn't changed at all — just like a suckling baby!"

After a moment's silence, he looked at her again. "This is the way life goes. It was raining exactly like this on the day I arrived here. There would be torrential rains on the day of my departure as well. These trees and plants these roaring waves of the sea, these surging clouds — everything will be the same. A steamer would arrive and one drama would be over…"

He looked at her in surprise: "Arrey, you're weeping!" She hid her face in both her hands. With a jerk, she turned and stood at a distance and then she ran and disappeared. It rained with noisy patter. The clouds thundered. The lighting crashed. Saket stood there with his mouth agape…

He had already received the order of transfer. The new engineer had not yet reported to take the charge. Hence it was finally decided to hand over the charge to the senior overseer. Saket's transfer was on promotion. He didn't feel as happy about his promotion as he should have…

There was a personal letter from Mr. Badhwani — "I wasn't surprised to read the report about the devotion with which you've carried out your work. That was what I had expected of you beforehand..."

Saket looked at all places here with the eyes of a stranger.

He took snaps of those places for Anni...

Nina wasn't seen any more. She hadn't been coming to work. There were no letters from Deep Di either. She had changed her residence. Now she had a new address. In her last letter, she wrote: "If you don't receive my letter for a long time if you stop getting letters from me, take it that Deep is dead...!"

Saket passed his time in a strange state of suspense. He hadn't been able to sleep for the past eight or ten days. Goodness knew what all he had been thinking! He wanted to finish all his jobs before leaving. The days were spent going from place to place. Then he had to attend to the office work till midnight.

The orderly was thinking — "Sahib hasn't been eating well for a long time. Nor is he sleeping properly. He doesn't even talk much. Perhaps he is impatient to get back. He hasn't gone home for more than three years!"

Saket's health had improved considerably after his last lung illness. But now it was the same again...

The cigarette continued burning and his eyes fixed in the void, seemed to be searching for something.

He would be leaving by the motorboat the next morning. It was almost midnight by the time his luggage was packed...

Everyone had gone off to sleep. The hurricane lantern was burning. He sat on a bench outside. He could see the seashore in the far distance. The sparkling waves were rolling over each other. He came inside but was unable to sleep. He just lay wearily on the bed.

He got up before daybreak. He waited with his luggage on the jetty. He had taken leave of everyone. They had all come to give a farewell. He had already spent the major portion of his salary. He had made some clothes for the children of the tribal labourers. He had bought for them books to study. He had also made arrangements for the medical treatment of the tribals…!

Everyone was there— only she was missing…!

He sat on the shore waiting for the motorboat! For Nina! Or for both! Or for neither!

Who could say when he would have a chance to come here again? or whether he would be able to come at all?

He thought about that innocent girl, who had none in the world to call her own…! White rows of teeth, a smiling face, the ash tied in a bundle, a roof about to collapse—everything floated before his eyes…

The morning passed. The afternoon also wore on, but the motorboat was nowhere in sight. The whole day passed in waiting.

The motorboat stopped near the jetty in the evening. The driver informed him that there was some trouble with the engine. It would need further repairs during the night. Only after that, they would be able to leave the next morning.

Saket returned to the camp with his luggage…

Nina was still nowhere to be seen. The labourers said she had probably gone away to some other Island…

Late in the evening, Saket went towards the tribal settlement. That shed was completely broken. The pillar too was missing. There was a broken earthen pot and also some rags lying around. There was a dry coconut in a corner and also remnants of some dry fish.

The moon was now partly visible. The sea was beginning to be rough. There was no boat in sight anywhere. The entire coast was deserted…

He wandered around aimlessly. Ultimately, when he was about to return, he saw a dark shape on the rock where he often used to sit.

Out of curiosity, he went closer. That dark shape grew larger:

Some rags fluttered in the air. And the dishevelled hair…

"Ni…!"

Nina didn't move. Her eyes were fixed on the steamboat anchored at the jetty. Her whole face was bruised. And there was no trace of emotion— as though it was smeared with ash!

"Nina!" he shook her violently.

Nina remained still as ever.

He shook her more violently.

"Ni...ni....!"

She stood up, as though she were in a trance.

She stared at him listlessly, as if she had just awakened from sleep.

"Ninni, what has happened to you?"

Nina dropped herself into his arms like a dead bird…

The Nicobari, Bihari…Oriya—all labourers were gathered on the shore again. They brought again with them the customary gifts of dried fish and coconuts.

It was already dawn.

On the deck—

Two faces, mad with joy, peered. Two pairs of hands simultaneously waved in the air.

TWELVE

The shore receded in the distance and finally could no longer be sighted. Nina sat on the chair and leaning against the railing of the deck was looking at the waves. Saket, lying on the easy chair, counted the birds flying in the clouded sky. She came closer and sitting on the armrest, of the chair asked: "Hungry?"

He blew a ring of cigarette smoke in the air, "Yes!"

She went inside and took a dry coconut. She banged it on the floor and broke it. She offered one piece to him. Saket broke it into two pieces, taking one piece towards his own mouth and the other towards her…

Nina had kept one gunny bag full of dry coconuts and areca nuts.

"Why have you brought all this?"

She smiled. She pointed at her tattered clothes: "To exchange at Akuji's shop."

Saket smiled to himself.

"Well, have you got the steamer fare?"

"No…!"

"Then I'll make you get off and throw you in the sea!"

She waved her hands and giggled: "No, no, no!"

Soon it was time for lunch.

Saket served a few things on two big plates. She emptied her share in Saket's plate: "No, you'll eat first!"

"No," Saket protested. "We'll eat together!" She too was adamant. On no account did she agree to eat with Saket from the same plate. She continued staring at her dirty hands. Her shyness, her innocent hesitation tickled him. After he finished eating, she drew that same plate towards herself and quickly gobbled everything.

Saket explained to her that she must eat slowly and nicely. Otherwise, people would think her uncivilized…

A small fan rotated on the ceiling of the cabin. She looked at it in wonder. Even during the day, she kept on switching on and switching off the electric lights. How did that light come and then, how it was pitch dark…!

She removed Saket's shoes. She collected the clothes lying scattered on the chair and hung them on the pegs. Every now and then, she held Saket's small watch to her ears.

The tick-tick sound and the moving of the needles appeared very mysterious to her.

When Saket stretched on the bed and started reading something, she also picked up a magazine. She saw the coloured pictures and tried to identify big letters. Saket gave her a pencil and asked her to write something. She wrote with great effort and then, like a little girl, read it very loudly.

Saket got up from sleep. He found that while he was sleeping, she had washed and dried her saree and put it on again! She had combed her hair in a new style. She looked very charming in her white saree.

After some time, she poured tea which had been kept in a tray. She extended one cup towards him.

"I hope it isn't cold?" Saket asked.

She checked it by dipping her finger: "No!"

"One doesn't do that!" Saket said and she felt embarrassed.

It would have been more convenient to go to Delhi via Madras, but Saket had some work in Port Blair. Hence he planned his voyage to go to Calcutta via Port Blair and then go from there to Delhi.

Nina was awe-struck by the city of Port Blair. Huge pucca buildings, big shops, cars, and all kinds of people moving on the roads. That new atmosphere astonished her.

Saket got new clothes for her. He bought slippers for her as well as other items of daily use. Nina just did not know what she would do with so many things! She protested — but was Saket the one to listen to her?

She found it very odd to walk with slippers on her feet.

Ever since Saket brought those things for her, Nina sat before the mirror the whole time. She made all sorts of faces and teased herself. She talked to herself and laughed all by herself.

Saket looked on at her odd movements like a dumb spectator. He said to himself that she looked really very lovely in her white saree without all those adornments.

He took Nina to a film in the Mountbatten Talkies. He also showed her the jail where the freedom fighters had been kept as life prisoners. Nina was fascinated by the Rose Island. An engineer known to Saket had come there last year to carry out construction work. It was nice to go around with his family. Nina had learnt to dress properly by that time. She had changed quite a lot in the past few days. She looked vastly different. Her characteristic ability to adjust herself to the circumstances proved to be extremely helpful.

After Port Blair, Saket stopped at Calcutta for two or three days. Nina felt lost in the surging crowds of that city. Her eyes opened wide when she looked at the endless rows of cars, trams and trains, And so many people! She wondered where so many people could be going at the same time. Somewhat scared, nervous and confused, she tried to look for herself in that vast human ocean.

She bought some toys for Anni, Chhaya and Roop with the pocket money Saket had given her.

"Arrey, toys for such grown-up children!" Saket tried to stop her, but she didn't listen to him. She said: "Children play only with toys. You said they are children. We must buy toys for children…!"

One day a taxi stopped at the door…

There were no special preparations to receive Saket since he had not intimated the definite date of his arrival.

Of course, Roop's study room had been vacated for him. The walls had been freshly whitewashed. Everyone had started living properly, lest Saket should get offended.

The moment the taxi's horn was heard, they all came out rushing and clung to Saket.

Panicked and shrinking within herself, Nina stepped out of the taxi. Everyone gave her an astonished look.

"Arrey, why are you standing there staring, Roop? She's your Bhabhi."

"Bhabhi!" Roop shrieked with laughter. "You're very bad Bhaiya. You didn't even inform us! Mamaji has selected four girls for you here — exactly four!"

All burst out laughing. Saket smiled: "What shall I do with four? Only one would suffice for us — what do you say?" He looked at Nina who blushed.

Roop led her Bhabhi into the house very respectfully and affectionately. She shouted right from the staircase: "Amma, see Bhaiya has come with our Bhabhi!"

Roop thumped noisily on the Amma's door which was closed from inside.

Amma came with a rosary in her hand.

"What's the matter?"

"Bhaiya has come — he has also brought Bhabhi with him…"

Amma raised her eyes. "Yes! she said and Nina at once tried to touch her feet. Amma didn't say anything. She just stepped back…"

Roop brought Nina to the sitting room…

Saket came out to wash his hands after finishing his meal. Scraping his teeth with a skewer, he asked: "How do you find your Bhabhi?"

"She's nice, Bhaiya, very nice…!" Roop couldn't contain her happiness. She couldn't decide what she should say. After a pause, she said just to irritate him: "Bhaiya, Anni says our Bhabhi is somewhat dark…"

Saket laughed aloud: "He's right… but tell me, what do you think?"

"I find her extremely nice! She talks very sweetly. She smiles while she talks. Such gleaming lovely teeth and I haven't seen anyone with such beautiful big eyes…" She said after a moment's silence: "Why don't we have such people around here, Bhaiya?"

Saket laughed: "What do you mean? What type of people?"

Roop was confused.

"Has Amma taken her meal, Roop? " Saket asked as he kept the water jug on the floor. As he started wiping his mouth with a towel, he suddenly remembered Deep Di…

"Amma is still having her bath, Bhaiya. She'll eat later."

"Is this the time to bathe?"

"Bhabhi and you touched her feet — that's why!" Saket smiled…

Saket didn't approve of Roop's behaviour towards Amma.

Roop snubbed her for every little thing…

Saket lay in his room smoking his cigarette. "Roop!" he called out.

Roop was having her meal. She got up at once and stood before him.

"Sit down!"

She sat on the teapoy in front of him. They sat silent for a while.

"How is Amma's health?"

"Not too good! She gets into too many tantrums."

Saket stared at the cigarette smoke. "What would be Amma's age now?"

"Well…she must be quite old."

"I think she won't live very long!" She started at him.

"It pained me to see it all!" he said, shaking off ash from his cigarette. "You shouldn't treat Amma like this. Did you behave in the same manner with her during my absence?.... I don't know if God exists or not! But if he did exist, He wouldn't be better than one's father and mother…!"

His voice choked. A few moments passed in grim silence. Roop got up and left…

Chhaya constantly clung to his legs. Anni had grown up a bit. He had become naughtier than before. Saket had brought lots of clothes for everyone from Calcutta — sarees for Roop and for Amma an expensive Pashmina shawl and innumerable icons for her to worship.

"Chhaya, you've grown taller even than me! I didn't recognize you at first. Who has come to the house, I said to myself!"

Hearing that. Anni laughed — Roop laughed too — only poor Chhaya stood there piqued.

"Now tell me, did you recognize me?"

"Yes!"

"From how far?"

"Very far…!"

"It means that now your eyes are fine. Roop, why did you tell a lie in your letter?"

Roop broke into a laugh.

"Well, tell me, does Roop beat you?" Saket asked.

"No…!"

"And this little beast?" he looked at Anni.

"Sometimes he grabs my share of eats and runs away…!"

"So, that's the thing! We'll fix him in his place!" Saket looked at Chhaya's eyes. "Now I'm back! Let me see how your eyes don't become all right! I'm sure Roop didn't take you to a doctor!"

Anni showed him his books as well as his result sheet.

Saket was very tired, but when he went to sleep, he couldn't sleep. The children were in such a pitiable state as though they were orphaned. During these few years, Amma's health had greatly deteriorated. And the state of the saree Roop had been wearing! Was the money he had been sending insufficient? How did they manage to live all those years…?"

Saket got up very late in the morning. He found Dada Babu standing in front of him.

"Engineer Babu, my respects…!" he sat on the durri and folded his hands.

Saket was dumbfounded. He got up and raising Dada Babu by his hand, made him sit on a chair.

"Dada Babu, you've aged so much in these three or four years! Your hair turned all grey like jute!"

Dada Babu bared his yellowed teeth and said: "It's a year since my wife died…!"

"Have you given up your job at the hosiery?"

"Yes, I lost heavily in that business."

"Then what's your business now?"

"I did lots of things, Engineer Babu. But then I gave up everything. I'm not able to sleep ever since my wife died. Hence, I've been working as a watchman in this mohalla. I managed to have two square meals…" Dada Babu said, "Engineer Babu, I've heard you've also brought a wife along!"

"Yes," Saket nodded his head.

"Then, no sweets and all that?"

"Why not?" Saket smiled: "The bride is still young, Dada Babu, and so, you'll get only a little sweet."

Saket burst into a hearty laugh.

Dada Babu bared his entire broken rows of teeth, "I had thought our Engineer Babu would become a big man and would open a 'factory' for me… Now Engineer Babu has brought a bride…He has come back safe from across the black water and now he talks of giving us only a little sweet...!" He opened a bundle which was tucked in his armpit. "Amma yaar, our Engineer Babu has come back home. We're happy. We'll distribute sweets!"

He started distributing sweets.

"Engineer Babu, there's light in the mohalla with your coming. I used to come here every day and ask: 'How is our Engineer Babu?' I always thought that if I died on the road, my Engineer Babu wouldn't let me remain unclaimed… Now Engineer Babu is not interested in…!" Dada Babu's eyes became moist.

THIRTEEN

"Bhaiya, did you see? Bhabhi has brought toys for me!"

Roop burst out laughing.

"So what? Have you grown very big or what?" He pulled her plait and lightly patted her cheek.

"Bhabhi has brought such a lot of betel-nuts — so much!" She extended both her arms. "Bhaiya, why should you be an Engineer and all that? Why don't you open a paan shop? Lime and catachew are the only things needed."

Saket pulled her plait hard and she squealed and laughed.

"Bhabhi doesn't know embroidering or knitting," she said, "She can only boil fish!"

"Arrey, she cooks the fish so well that you'll bite your fingers while you eat the fish! But yes, if you bite your fingers, how can you be married?"

Both Anni and Chhaya started laughing.

"What's Bhabhi's name, Bhaiya?"

Saket was silent for a while and said: "You ask her."

"But she doesn't say anything."

"Then I too won't say."

"Please, say! You didn't even send the marriage card!" She said insistently. There was a picture of the river on the opposite wall. The moment Saket saw that picture something flashed in his mind.

"I've named your Bhabhi 'Ganga'."

"Why 'Ganga'?"

"Ganga is the great river, you know. It covers the whole earth with greenery. It is a sacred river…!"

Roop said in a chirping voice: "Our aunt at school used to tell us that King Bhagirath had brought the Ganga down to the earth from heaven. She said Bhagirath was a well-known engineer of his time. In that sense, you too have become Bhagirath!" and she laughed aloud as she clapped her hands. "But our Bhabhi's name should be not Ganga but Yamuna, Bhaiya! She is really like the Yamuna river—dark!"

Saket couldn't help laughing.

"You've become so intelligent after attending school just for a couple of years! I wonder what would have happened if you had studied for a few years more!"

Laughter burst forth like a spring.

All the women of the mohalla came one by one, like a row of ants, together with their children. Only one thing was being talked about everywhere — that Saket had brought a girl from the jungles of the Andamans! Her large eyes were like bows and her teeth gleamed extremely bright. She had very sharp features, but her complexion was absolutely dark. She could speak Hindi and do household chores. Ever since she came, Saket's mother had started plastering her room with cow dung twice a day. She had been keeping her room closed from the inside after sprinkling cow's urine. Formerly she had been bathing half a dozen times in a day, but now she was under the tap the whole time! In case she died of pneumonia, the whole mohalla would incur the blame for it!...

"They say, in that place, man eats man! It's very risky to bring home such a girl."

"And listen dear sister, our Tirloki says that men and women go about naked over there— how would she have lived there!" and they started giggling.

"Arrey, that's not all! It's written in the books that all the people in that place know black magic! Who can say if she has cast a spell on Saket too!"

They talked about all sorts of things — just about anything they pleased.

There were so many people crowding the house all through the day that Saket just didn't know what to do.

Saket's leave period was about to get over. He would have to resume attending office... There was no improvement in Chhaya's eyes. Once in a way, she went to school just like that. Saket thought to himself that no matter what happened, her eyes had to be operated upon. He was furious with himself that he had not been able to arrange for her treatment so far. What would happen if she lost her eyes altogether?

He got up and went inside. Roop had to the market. Chhaya was groping for something in a corner. He went to the terrace. "Nina!"

She was startled.

"What are you doing here seated all by yourself?"

She shook her head and said with a smile: "Nothing!"

"Will you come with me for a walk?"

"Where?"

"To the seaside where a new jetty is coming up."

She smiled and gazed at him.

"Come on soon it will be night. I've some important thing to do."

She started getting ready.

Saket came down and stood waiting for her. Nina could not be recognized when she got dressed to go out. Her shapely slim body was wrapped in a white silk saree, her Nicobari hairdo and no jewellery at all on her person. Nothing artificial about her. The same old simple smile on her lips and dreams that would emerge only from eyes — dreams, only dreams!

Saket gazed at her spellbound.

Saket had a basket in his hands which was full of big brown paper packets.

"Where shall we go?" she asked.

"Nowhere in particular."

Both of them laughed for no reason. A solitary eucalyptus tree stood there as always.

Saket climbed the stairs of a building alone. He knocked at the door. Even though it had grown dark, there was no light there.

He knocked at the door again.

He heard the sound of a chair being shifted on the floor and some muttering inside. And then slowly the door opened.

"Who is it?"

"It is me!"

"Who…Saket!" Deep Di gathered him in her arms.

"Arrey, you've come here at this time!"

"When would I come otherwise?" he said with the same old familiar smile.

Both went inside. The light was switched on. Saket found Deep Di changed beyond recognition. A melancholy face, dry hair, a coarse white khadi saree! Deep Di looked like a widow.

"You can't even recognise, Deep Di!"

"Of course, why you would recognize me? Only now you've found time to come here?"

"No, that's not the point."

"What do you mean?" Deep Di sighed heavily. "I say, why are you standing? Sit down."

"I've got someone with me!" he looked at her in confusion.

"Then call him up!"

Saket went down the stairs and came up again. This time, not one, but two faces peeped in.

Deep Di stood there astounded.

"This is our Deep Di. Arrey, pay your respects to her!"

While Nina bent low, Deep Di raised her hands and took her in her arms.

"You're so bad, I say! You didn't even tell me!"

Saket felt embarrassed.

"Arrey, why are you standing? Do sit down!" Deep Di said and they sat down.

"I heard that you had arrived yesterday, but you're showing your face now," Deep Di said in a reprimanding tone.

"It's not that, Deep Di! Ask her!"

"Why should I ask her — I'm asking you!" Deep Di said after a moment's silence added: "Now why don't you say you're going by the night train today?"

Saket laughed: "No, Deep Di! I'm not going so soon! I'm going to be around till you don't drive me out— one whole month! One year! Can't say how long!"

Before Deep Di could say anything, Saket quickly said: "You're scared at the mention of one year, isn't it? Now we're going to park ourselves here! What are you thinking about? You used to feed one person before, now you'll have to feed two!"

Saket laughed aloud and Deep Di had to laugh with him.

There were a few moments of silence. Deep Di glanced frequently at the lean innocent girl seated in front of her.

"Will you just sit like that or get us tea etc. ...?"

Now that Saket reminded her. Deep Di realised she had not even offered tea…

"Will you have tea or something else?"

"We'll have both, Deep Di!" He teased her as he used to do.

"First tea and then something else!"

They all laughed.

Soon tea was ready. Expecting Saket's visit, she had ordered sweets right since morning. She took a piece of barfi and fed Nina with her own hands. Without any formality, Saket went on swallowing pieces of barfi one after the other. He smiled when Nina told him not to eat like that. "You don't know our Deep Di, Nina! Whatever I'm today, is all due to her efficiency and good wishes…" As he said that, Saket grew suddenly serious.

Deep Di too was lost in some thought. Then she said: "Yes, why didn't you inform me? Arrey, you could have at least sent the wedding card!"

"I was so involved in hectic work in that jungle that I didn't find time at all! I swear by your name, Deep Di, it so happened that…!"

"Of course, now you'll even swear by my name!" Deep Di gulped her tea.

Saket laughed and his tea spilt from his cup.

"What could I have written to you when in every letter of yours you talked only about dying? Do you remember that towards the end you had even avoided giving your address?"

"Who can stand before you when it comes to using words? I acknowledge my defeat!" After a pause, Deep Di asked: "How far has your wife studied?"

"She's a graduate of the Kabir University, Deep Di!"

"I see! What were her subjects for her B.A.?"

"There's a great difference between the studies here and the studies there."

"Yes, indeed it should be different," Deep Di said unthinkingly.

"What do her parents do?"

"Nothing, Deep Di! just spend their time doing nothing!" Saket said laughing. "You think I'm lying? No, I'm telling you the truth!"

Deep Di suddenly laughed for no reason.

After a little chit-chat, Saket got up: "We must leave now. I've to buy medicine for Chhaya. Shops would close otherwise."

"But what's the hurry now?" Deep Di asked.

"But we would be coming tomorrow!" And Saket held out the basket for her.

"What's in the basket?"

"Nothing. Just keep it…!"

They left after promising Deep Di to have lunch with her the following day which happened to be Sunday. Deep Di came rushing from inside with a few old notes in her fist and put them in Nina's hand.

"What's this?"

"You keep quiet! The daughter-in-law has come here for the first time…!"

"Will you give her the same amount every time she comes?"

Deep Di pretended to be angry and then burst into a laugh.

They came down the stairs and disappeared at the bend of the street. Deep Di stood on the balcony watching them and then came inside, lost in some thought…

Deep Di had done no other work since morning. She finished cooking and waited. It was nearing one o'clock, but Saket hadn't come yet. She kept on walking — outside, and then inside…!

Lunch had already gone cold. Deep lighted the coal stove again and came out—and there Saket stood before her.

"You've come alone!"

"Yes, she was busy at home."

"In that case, you should have arrived on time…!"

"You're right," Saket said. "I was indeed telling Nina that Deep Di's lunch period' must have started...!" He looked at Deep Di and realized that she was really offended.

He realized that it would be dangerous to make any more noise. Hence, he removed his shoes and stretching his legs, stretched himself on the sofa. Perhaps he had come hurrying— maybe running.

Deep Di started laying the plates on the table. Finally, after keeping the jug of water she stood hesitating before him. "Have you gone to sleep?"

Without moving, he just opened his eyes.

"Your eyes have become red — I hope your health is all right?"

"I'm all right," he slowly sat up. "I'm having a slight headache, that's all."

Deep Di sat on the sofa by this side. She kept her hand on his forehead to check if he had a fever. "Yes, your forehead is hot. Will you take an Anacin?"

Saket declined.

They sat down for lunch. Saket ate in silence with his head lowered.

"Why did you get late?" Deep Di asked.

"Just like that. Amma got suddenly ill."

"Or did she start banging the utensils again?"

"Yes, something like that. She gets into those fits now and then. Yesterday, Anni burnt his hand on the stove. Today, when Chhaya slipped on the stairs, Amma got furious with Nina. She said, 'Ever since you've stepped in this house, all sorts of ominous things have been happening. The whole house has become contaminated'…" Saket's hands stopped on the plate.

Deep Di kept staring at him. She made no comment.

"Oh, yes, I've heard that you've got promoted," Deep Di observed to change the course of the conversation.

"Yes."

"How long will you be on leave?"

"Another month or so."

"Have you got your transfer here?"

"I'll be here for the time being."

"I had heard you had fallen very sick?"

"Yes, I had been getting some fever, that's all."

"How is the climate there?"

Saket was silent. Then he said: "Good."

"Take more roti!"

"No, no! I had enough. I just had my breakfast."

Deep Di forcibly put one roti on Saket's plate.

After finishing lunch, Saket dipped his fingers in the glass to clean them. While he got up looking for a towel something suddenly flashed in his mind. He pulled out a handkerchief from his pocket and wiped his face.

After a while, Deep Di brought two cups of tea.

"What's this?"

"You used to take tea after lunch, didn't you?"

Saket had forgotten that there was a time when he used to take tea after lunch. That was a long time ago.

Drawing the cup towards himself Saket said: "You've changed a great deal, Deep Di!"

Deep Di's gaze was fixed on the teacup. A trembling wisp of steam rose from the cup.

"You look almost like a Sanyasini! I couldn't recognize you at first."

"Yes, you're right."

"Are you in the same old college?"

"Yes."

"I'm sure you never went home?"

Deep Di shook her head.

There are two or three pictures of some Gods on the racks by the side of the time-piece. On one of the pictures hung a Tulsimala.

"You've started doing pujas, is it?"

Deep Di didn't reply.

"Now we're living in a big house. One room on the upper floor is absolutely unoccupied. You're living here all by yourself. Nina said yesterday that you should shift there. She too would feel happy."

Deep Di heaved a sigh. "She is right. But I like being alone. I'm scared of crowds. I've lived all these years like this. I'll pass the rest of my life in the same way."

Saket had given time to somebody for a meeting at home. He looked at his watch.

When he started going, Deep Di came after him. Breaking the silence, she said: "I don't wish anything more — except that when you pass this way, do look me up. I would then feel reassured that there is at least someone who thinks about me—even if he has strayed...!"

Saket turned round with a jerk. Keeping his hands on her shoulders he said: "Why do you think like that, Deep Di?" His whole body trembled.

Deep Di said nothing in reply. She bit her lips and looked at him with tearful eyes.

"..."

"I'm really fed up with life, Saket. I don't understand why I'm living. For what purpose? For whom, after all?"

Deep Di started sobbing like a child: The sleeve of Saket's coat became wet...

"Will you come, Roop?"

"No, Bhaiya, Please take Bhabhi with you. I'm not fond of seeing films"

Saket pulled her plait: "You liar! Yesterday you yourself wanted to see a picture with me!"

Roop burst out laughing. She gave him a mischievous look: "I was joking. Today you two go and see a film!"

"Where is Nina?"

"She is cleaning utensils."

Nina was busy the whole day cleaning utensils. Roop said the other day: "Bhabhi has so cleaned all the utensils that they sparkle like glass. Now there's no need to do tin-plating for the utensils. And the floor is absolutely clean. As soon as she gets up in the morning, she cleans the entire threshold"

"Well, aren't we going?" Saket asked and Nina replied with her usual smile.

"Not going!"

"Look here, I shall start my work after my leave is over. I won't have time even to drink water. That's why I'm saying, whatever outings you wish to have, let's have them now. Don't blame me later."

Roop forced Nina to get ready.

Once she was ready, Roop tickled her and said: "You don't want to go! You don't know Hindi… Isn't that so? Bhabhi…?"

Nina was taken aback when Roop laughed. She quietly set out with Saket. Anni also wanted to accompany them, but Roop stopped him.

Deep Di who was buying vegetables, noticed two figures on the other side of the road. A taxi halted in front of them.

"How do you like this city?" he asked while sitting in the taxi.

"Not better than you!" She rested her head on his shoulder and closed her eyes.

FOURTEEN

Saket didn't realize how time had passed so quickly. The day began and soon it was evening! And even the evenings were so short...!

Chhaya had been admitted to the hospital...Mr. Badhwani passed away in Hyderabad following a cardiac arrest. It was said he had left his entire property for an orphanage... Rattan had got a job at Bhilai where he had taken his mother along...

Mamaji constantly complained: "Why did you many outside our own community? I had selected for you girls from good families. There's a businessman in our community who promised to give two trucks and even a house as dowry. The girl would have come to us laden with gold and silver..."

Saket smiled as he thought about all those things ...

Mamaji was fond of having betelnuts. He always kept a nutcracker in his pocket. He had taken away a bagful of betelnuts with him. He was no less happy that his only nephew had returned safe and sound from the Andamans. In his life, he was the first man he had known to return home across the Black Waters. He insisted that it was only the result of die Durga-Saptasati recitation he had arranged...

"Bhaiya, you aren't eating well these days. What's the matter?" Roop asked.

Saket replied with a smile: "I eat such nice things when I go to Connaught Place in the evening that when I return home, I don't feel like eating your dry rotis..."

"In that case, I too will accompany you from tomorrow."

"Did I ever forbid you? But if you come with me, we'll go walking and come home after taking a glass of cold water!"

Roop made a face at him. Then she said after some thought: "Bhabhi has only two sarees, Bhaiya. It's a blot on the Engineer Sahib's name!"

Saket smiled: "Two are too many. Actually, she should have only one." Then giving a light knock on her head he said: "There are millions of women in the country. On average, they may not have even two sarees. This engineer sahib will live like those women! An engineer is no God, is he?"

It was Sunday, Deep Di was attending to some college work at home. Her slightly wet hair was spread over her back. In the kitchen, rice was boiling on the stove. In between, she went in to check. She had lowered the flame and covered the vessel with a lid.

Suddenly Saket barged in shouting from the stairs: "What are you doing, Deep Di? Haven't you finished cooking yet? I'm hungry."

Promptly, Deep Di set aside her work. She noticed Nina also coming behind him with a smile. She was carrying a long paper bag in her hand containing a wrapped object.

"What have brought in this?"

"It's a charming thing not from Bengal but Nicobar. Deep Di!"

"What did you say?"

"Oh, oh! Why are you startled? You blow air from there and I'll change this into a cat here!" Saket said very seriously. Then with a dramatic gesture, he took out that thing from the paper bag and removed the newspaper wrapping. Finally, he produced a fish!

"You see, this Nina, I mean your Nina — she complained that she hadn't eaten fish ever once she came here. And what's a meal without fish? Once I said by mistake that my Deep Di made a lovely fish curry. Since then she has been insisting…"

Deep Di shook her head: "I understand everything — it's only your mischief!"

"Actually, the thing is like this, Deep Di. We can't cook fish at home. You know Amma's nature. Now you tell me, who else in the world except my Deep Di can cook it for us with love and feed us and while leaving we could even tell her bluntly that it was badly cooked and say you don't even know how to cook!"

Nina laughed. Deep Di laughed. All laughed.

"You aren't offended Deep Di, are you? If that's the case, we'll leave. Come, Nina, let's go!"

Deep Di merely gave him an angry look, without saying anything.

"Go, Nina, get a glass of water!" he said to Nina.

Nina brought a glass of water which Saket offered to Deep Di. "Here, drink this water. It'll cool your temper."

After a brief pause, Saket looked at Deep Di and said: "This was a mere pretext, Deep Di. Actually, we decided that we should all eat together today. You would never come to our house. So, we thought we would put aside all our sense of shame and come here. It's such a long time — did you ever invite us for a meal?"

Deep Di looked at him with a strange expression. Leaving the scattered notebooks as they were, she went inside. It was as though something had touched her to the very core and a groaning cry rose inside her.

"What's your programme today, Deep Di?"

"Nothing particular. I've to attend to some college work!"

"The college work can be done even at night. A poor man that I am, I've got only one saree for you— I've given one to Roop… I'm joining office from tomorrow. Then I won't have any time. So. why don't you come and buy a saree for her? They say your tastes are very good!"

"You two go and buy. Why do you want to drag me?"

"What will you do sitting here alone? We shall sit somewhere for coffee, and come back after buying the saree. That's all!"

Saket forced Deep Di to get ready. They sat in a restaurant for some time and had coffee.

Saket bought a saree of Deep Di's choice — not one but two of the same type— and had them packed in separate packets. While returning home he insisted on presenting one of the sarees to Deep Di and left the packet on her table…

FIFTEEN

The same routine again — leaving home in the morning and returning late at night. And then, working at home till the late hour of the night... Nina would be seated looking out from the balcony.

She too sat hungry till Saket didn't eat. When Saket returned home after a tired day's work, she would fix her melancholy eyes on him...

"Have you taken your dinner?" he asked, removing his coat and keeping it aside.

"I'll eat. What's the hurry? Sitting at home, I don't even feel hungry."

She sat at his feet and started removing his shoes. "Your feet are so hot!" She said and went on stroking his feet.

"When Nina started warming up the food, Saket shouted from his room: "Why bother to warm up the food? Just bring it as it is. Is this the time to eat and keep awake?"

But Nina didn't listen.

She served him the dinner very affectionately. "Now, will you get up or let it go cold again?"

Saket broke a piece of roti, "Arrey, what are you looking at? Why don't you also eat?"

"No, I'll eat later..."

Saket looked at her. "Indeed! If you also eat now, who will take count of how many morsels I have taken? You must have something to quarrel about! Yesterday I ate half a roti less. Today one less!..."

Saket was very hungry. He ate his food and continued talking at the same time — without waiting for her reaction.

In spite of his protests, Nina kept roti and cooked vegetables on his plate.

"If I eat more, I sleep more and the work suffers…"

Nina didn't say anything. She only sat before him folding in her legs.

While Nina went in to get some more rotis, Saket dipped his fingers in the glass. He slid the plate on one side, jumped on to his bed and scattered the plans and other papers around him, lost himself amidst the pile.

He didn't hear what Nina said. Absent-mindedly, he kept on replying in monosyllables like 'Yes' and 'No'.

"You must be feeling sleepy. Go to bed," he said raising his head from the pile of those papers. "You work the whole day. You must be getting tired!"

She remained seated silently in the same position. Then she went to another room and picking up a book, started reading herself. She had learnt quite a lot during those few days.

While reading, she started dozing. Then she came to Saket's room to check. He had folded his arms over the edge of the bed and resting his forehead on them was lost in some thought.

She stroked his head. Then she put her hand to his forehead — it was hot.

"Shall I press your forehead?"

"No."

"Sure you're not having a fever?" She held his wrist. "I think you have a slight fever!"

While applying balm on his forehead, she gently switched off the bed light.

It was past two o'clock…

Every morning, while leaving for office he said to Nina: "Go for an evening walk with Roop. You must be feeling bored sitting at home!"

Once he looked around the room, and drawing Nina close to himself said: "You've gone very lean. Don't you feel at home here?"

She was silent.

"Then what's the matter?"

She didn't say anything. Instead, she simply went on turning the button of his coat…

Once in a way, Saket came home early. Occasionally, he took Nina with him to some party, with the idea that she would feel more free by mixing with people. But Nina remained aloof like oil on the surface of the water. She did make an effort to mix with people but couldn't do it. Sometimes she spilled tea from the cup or spoiled her saree with ice cream or forgot to pick up her purse…

One day, Saket returned late at night. He found Nina seated alone on the dark terrace, her gaze fixed at the sky.

"Nina!"

Nina came close and clung to him.

"Is this the time to come home?"

Patting her lightly he said: "Now look, I'm very hungry today."

Both of them came down.

"Just see, what I've brought for you?" he held out a packet to her.

She kept it aside carefully. "Have your dinner first. We can talk later…"

"What's the hurry about having dinner?"

"You just said you were very hungry!"

Saket laughed. "Really, you're so innocent! I said that just to please you…"

Nina smiled.

"What did you do during the day?" Saket asked.

Like a little girl, she brought her notebook and counted the pages: "I wrote this much."

"What else?"

She brought out thick white sheets of paper from the almirah.

"What's this?"

There was a pencil drawing of coconut trees.

"These trees…"

"They are the coconut trees, aren't they?"

"And this thing at the bottom?" he looked at it very closely.

"Didn't you recognize? It's the jetty — yes, jetty!"

"Oh, yes, it's indeed the jetty. Exactly like what we had built."

The rows of her crystal-like teeth sparkled. She went on nodding her head. "Yes, yes!"

"This is wonderful! You've drawn the boats as well! I never imagined you were such a remarkable artist too!"

Nina felt unbounded joy when he praised her so highly.

After dinner, Saket opened that packet.

"What's this?"

Saket asked her to bring a glass of water and a couple of small bowls. He mixed the paints and started colouring Nina's plain drawings.

Nina looked on with astonishment. Soon those ordinary-looking thin black lines came to life. The whole picture became lively. Lush green coconut trees, heaving blue sea. grey, cloudy sky! She felt a fragrance emanating from the earth-sweet pleasant fragrance of the earth! The smell of the fish swimming in the water! The fragrance of the blue forest flowers! The sweet tunes of the fishermen's music that continued all through the night… Nina kept her palms on her ears and closed her eyes.

SIXTEEN

Nina had changed a lot. She looked quite different after her one-year stay here. Her sanskaras of the past were all gone. One could not make out that she had ever lived in Nicobar. She spoke in a very chaste language. She read newspapers every day. She observed fasts. She went and bought things from the market. She attended to all household chores.

She was no longer the restless creature she had been once. She had now acquired a serious mind. She spoke only when necessary. She served Amma in the best possible manner... Chhaya's eyes now showed great improvement. She couldn't read and write even though she had grown so big! Hence, Nina spent a lot of time teaching her, how to read and write.

One day, Saket informed her that his name was included among the engineers who were being sent to America for special training. He would have to stay there for about a year.

Nina brought down the map of the world which hung on the wall. Saket showed her the place by passing his finger over it.

"Will you go by car?"

"No!"

"Then by train?"

"No!"

"Then by steamer?"

"Oh, no, I'll go by plane!"

Nina asked no further questions and gazed at the outlines on the map.

The next day Saket found that Nina had drawn a very big map of America. With the point of his pen, he made a dot on the map to indicate the place where he would be staying.

Nina hung the map on the wall.

The date of his departure was fixed. Saket was making the necessary preparations. Putting his clothes in the attache he said: "Why don't you say something?"

"What should I say?" Nina tried to smile.

"What shall I bring for you from America?"

"I don't want anything except yourself."

"You mean you don't want food or clothes!" Saket continued packing his clothes in the attache. "You've become a real devotee of God! When somebody says he doesn't want anything, he has become king of kings!" Then closing the attache with a click he stared at her face. "So, you don't want anything, right?" he said aloud.

Nina burst out laughing.

Saket remarked in a mischievous tone: "You've laughed today after ages! Surely something untoward will happen today!" and he too laughed like her. "If it rains today, it will definitely rain fish! Just see!"

"If one wants to talk tall, it must be learnt from you!" Nina made a face.

"Now listen," Saket got up and came to her. "When we build the bridges and the roads and set up factories, we shall have to talk tall, isn't it?"

Saket peered into her eyes, "Your eyes look swollen!"

"They are not swollen. I've put on a lot of weight these days, you know!"

A voice, free like a brook, filled the air once again.

The taxi was parked at the turn of the road. Saket found Deep Di's house locked. Three months had gone by since she went to Kanpur! During that period, there was no letter, no information! Of course, her niece Prabha did write to say that her Mausi was ill.

No further information since then.

Saket looked at his watch. There was very little time left. He asked the taxi driver to drive fast. The taxi picked up speed and turned towards the Palam airport.

"Do write letters, right?"

Nina nodded her head.

"Write everything in detail. And take particular care of Amma. Don't feel hurt by whatever she may say… And look after Chhaya's eyes. I'm worried about Roop's marriage. I could not fix it… Let me know if there is any letter from Deep Di…One year — it won't be long before one year is over…"

Nina nodded her head like a little girl. Her face was sad. She hadn't eaten anything since the previous day. Saket had noticed that during the night she had been weeping hiding her face on the pillow.

Saket kept his hand on her drooping shoulder. He drew her close to himself: "You're very sentimental. It's no good being too sentimental…

Shadows appeared and vanished in her sad eyes. So many pictures are formed and wiped out…

Mamaji had already reached the airport with Roop, Chhaya and Anni.

It was time for departure. They all stood resting on the railing. A big Air India plane could be seen at a distance. People were proceeding hurriedly with their baggage forming some sort of a queue.

Saket was carrying a heavy bag in his hand. He carried a black overcoat with him. As he walked ahead, he repeatedly looked back and waved his hand climbing ten or fifteen steps of the ladder, disappeared through the cave-like entrance…

She walked up and down in the house. She just didn't know what to do. She didn't feel at home anywhere.

"Bhabhi, let's go and see a movie today, I've got two tickets." Roop showed her two tickets. But Nina didn't seem to take any notice of them.

But ultimately she had to go despite herself.

She had very strange dreams at night. She suddenly woke up and discovered that there was no plate on the teapoy in which she served dinner to Saket…

Each moment was like an age for Nina. She wondered how one whole year would pass.

Saket's letters arrived at short intervals in the beginning. But gradually the intervals grew longer. Finally, the letters became very formal just a few lines…!

There were no good medical facilities in Kanpur. Even otherwise, Deep Di wasn't at ease there. It was quite irksome to live for long with some distant relatives. In that state of mind, she wrote a letter to Saket saying that she wished to go over to Delhi for her medical treatment. But so many days passed in waiting for his reply…!

When she returned to Delhi alone and thoroughly disappointed, she found a letter inside near the door. It had foreign stamps and Saket's handwriting.

"I could not meet you before leaving. How is your health? Do write…"

Except for these few words, there was nothing else in the letter — absolutely nothing!

Nina wrote one letter to him every week. She wrote, "Why don't you reply to my letters? I wait for the postman every day. I have kept on the terrace a coconut wrapped in a red cloth. No misfortune will visit us now…I am keeping twice as many fasts as before…"

Saket read those letters and kept them aside.

How long does it take for a year to pass? Finally, Saket did return home one day. But Nina saw that he was not the same Saket he had been before. How much he had changed! Of course, he now looked much healthier and smarter. He had acquired a charming personality.... and how clothes and other things he had brought with him…!

"You can't even be recognized. Ninni You've become so lean!" he said with surprise.

Nina stared at him.

"Why have you become dumb? Have you forgotten to speak?" he raised her chin.

"It seems you passed all these days without sleeping and eating. Isn't that so?"

Nina's eyes brimmed with tears. With all her efforts, she could utter no word. She had really become dumb!

SEVENTEEN

Saket had now been given a higher position. The scope of his work had expanded. Formerly even while in Delhi, he couldn't find any spare time. But now he had to rush to Calcutta and Bombay as well. And at home, the telephone bell rang constantly. Saket would be in one place today, and somewhere else the next day!

Nina had decided that when Saket returned, she would have a series of complaints: "Why did you write such letters? Why didn't you reply to my letters in time? I had frightening dreams when you had injured your hand. The moment I closed my eyes, I saw only you standing in front of me…!"

But she never got an opportunity to have a leisurely chat with him. She would finish cooking and wait. And then Saket would telephone: "You have your meal. I've already eaten something in the office. There's no time for me to come home!"

Nina found it hard to swallow even one morsel of food. But if she didn't eat, Saket lost his temper.

She thought: "Today we shall go out." She hadn't stepped out of the house for many days. When she telephoned Saket urging him to come early, he expressed his helplessness and quietly placed back the receiver…

Then all of a sudden, the office peon came and said: "Sahib is going on tour to Calcutta for five days. He wants you to keep his luggage ready."

Nina silently started packing his luggage.

Saket came home in a hurry. He caressed Nina and said: "I shall definitely come back on Tuesday. Then we shall surely have an outing?"

Nina smiled ironically.

From Calcutta, Saket Trunk called to say that he was going to Bombay and would be back by the fifteenth…

Nina was very perturbed…

Nina stood in the doorway when Saket was leaving for the office: "Will you listen to me at least sometimes or…"

Saket turned back and looked at her. He gently pressed her drooping shoulders. "Tell me, if not you, whom would I listen to? You exercise the greatest power over me!"

Nina was silent.

"Tell me! Will you say something or just…"

Nina hid her head on his chest. Saket became suddenly grim: "All your complaints are justified. But what can I do? My life has become so mechanical…!"

He stroked her dishevelled hair. Holding her face between his palms, he smothered her with kisses.

When Saket started going down the stairs, Roop called him out: "Bhaiya, come home early today! Bhabhi is observing a fast."

Saket came home on time carrying in his both hands paper bags full of fruits.

"Today it was a day of fasting not only for you but also for me. I could find no time throughout the day to have my lunch!" Saket said aloud from a distance finding Nina standing on the stairs.

Nina took those bags from Saket's hands and walked behind him. Then keeping them on the table, she untied the laces of his shoes.

"I think you must be fasting every day. You tell me just to fool me that you eat in this place and that place…" Nina said petulently. "After all, for whom are you working so hard?"

"For ourselves, for the country! If even people like us don't work hard and honestly, who else would? You don't understand, Ninni!" he jerked his head and became silent.

"Your feet are so warm! And see how the veins are standing out! Shall I wash them with salted water? It would really give great relief."

"No, no. You quickly finish your meal. Then we shall go out up to the temple."

They came out of the house. They walked leisurely and on the way, stopped in front of Deep Di's house. They saw some clothes hanging on the clothesline and found the house locked from outside…

The car glided like a fish along Bela Road. Saket himself was at the wheel. Nina sat by his side. The car moved on and turned towards Connaught Place. They felt a jerk at the turning.

The car passed the Parliament Street and moved on. It finally stopped in front of the entrance of a grand building of a club. The green neon light on the building blinked…

The corner in which Saket was seated got gradually filled. Countless, figures, fragrant like flowers, moved all around. Nina stared at them…

Saket was dressed in khadi clothes as usual. People burst into guffaws at everything he said. Politics, religion, sex— he talked with authority on every subject…

People went on guzzling mug-full of beer, but Saket had a glass of fruit juice in front of him. He offered one glass to Nina and put the other glass to his lips. People doubled up with laughter when they heard him narrate his amusing and interesting experiences in America.

The orchestra was being played in front of them. A semi-naked woman was singing an English song, swaying on her legs, her eyes moving coquettishly as she sang. She swayed her broad buttocks in a very obscene manner…

A little later, the ball dance began. Men and women started dancing with their arms around each other's waist. Suddenly, a rosy woman, lean and tall, came close to Saket. She smiled and prodded him to get up. Saket begged to be excused.

The woman went away making the same wiggle-waggle movement.

Saket sat in glum silence for a while. Then, as though something had suddenly flashed in his mind, he looked at Nina and said: "You be seated. Have coffee. I shall soon be back," and he walked towards the counter.

The coffee was served. Nina waited for Saket for a long time. Then she poured a cup for herself and started sipping. The cup slowly emptied. She couldn't decide what she should do next.

She came out and stood on the balcony.

There were long rows of cars extending far into the distance. On the road opposite the cars moved in an undulating line. She was attracted by their lights creating several angles. But soon her attention was diverted from there also.

The dark green colour of the lawn appeared somewhat black. Nina saw two dim figures on the grass near the car-park area. One of them appeared to be a man, the other a tall woman. The man was probably smoking a cigarette. A tiny glow was visible in the distance.

When her legs got tired after standing so long, she came inside and sat down in the original seat. She noticed Saket entering through the door. A cigarette burnt between his fingers — like an ember.

After returning home, Nina kept on looking at her face in the mirror.

That night, she couldn't sleep a wink.

EIGHTEEN

The phone rang early in the morning. Nina passed on the receiver to Saket. Saket kept talking for a long time. There was someone's sweet voice at the other end. Saket repeatedly broke into laughter. And he constantly smiled. Finally, bursting into a guffaw, he said: "Yes, O.K." and put back the receiver with a click…

Saket came home very late that night. The car was damaged. It had been lying in the workshop since morning. Nina got tired, waiting alone inside. She constantly yawned and kept looking at the clock.

She tried to sleep, but sleep evaded her.

She brought a chair to the balcony and sat there. Leaning on the railing she went on counting the stray cars that rushed past.

And then a wave-like light came closer and piercing through darkness, stopped at the turn of the road. Nina saw that car turned after blowing the horn and stopped near the main gate. A man got down from the seat close to the driver. Then the car slowly turned back. A bare fair hand moved out from the driver seat. Thin delicate fingers moved… "Ta…Ta…!"

In response, the man entering through the gate turned back and looked that way, waving his hand.

Slow whirring and two blazing lights disappeared in the darkness…

Roop's final examination was to start from the fifth of the month. Nina said to Saket: "We must get some clothes for her. The poor girl is so simple she never asks for anything. This is the time for her to enjoy and have fun. Once she is married…"

Saket showed his helplessness. Again he explained how busy he was. He left some money with her and told Nina to go and make the purchases sometime during the day.

Nina could not refuse. She went to Connaught Place in the evening with Roop.

While walking through the corridor, Nina's eyes remained stuck on somebody's back. It was somebody like Saket. The same clothes, and he walked exactly like him with long strides. He was accompanied by a young woman — dressed in a light blue saree and blouse of the same colour and a charming hairdo.

They disappeared in some very big shop.

The next day, Nina wore a similar sky blue saree and blouse of the same colour and combed her hair in the same style. She applied lipstick to her lips and sat waiting for Saket till midnight.

Saket returned home late. Nina switched on all lights in the room and half reclining against the cushion smiled and looked at him as though asking: "Tell me, how do I look?"

Saket came to her like a wild beast. He tried to crush her between his arms but Nina jerked herself away from him and moved back.

"Arrey, you've even taken drinks today! Oh, God!...!"

Nina wriggled and shrieked. And then something came over Saket and he gave her a smarting slap.

Nina saw stars fleeting before her eyes. Her head whirled and she slumped on the floor unconscious…

The house appeared changed. There were no tables and chairs in the room. Some books lay scattered here and there. Deep Di was seated on the mat she had spread on the floor. She was playing with her spinning wheel.

"What would you gain by playing a spinning wheel in this scientific age, Deep Di?"

"It would not make an atomic bomb, Saket: But yes, some clothes would certainly be made to cover my body, what do you say?" Deep Di gave him an ironical look.

Saket stared silently at Deep Di. Deep Di's face no longer had that former glow. She had been wearing thick glasses. There was nothing in the room except a few things that were absolutely necessary.

"I hear that you've stopped working at your college?"

"Yes, in a way I've left it for good."

"Then what do you do for a living?"

"I give tuition to some children. My time passes. What more does a lonely creature like me need?" Deep Di said with a sense of detachment and then fell silent. After some thought, she said: "It's long since you came back from America. How often did you come during this period? How often did you inquire whether I was alive or dead? Nina used to come here sometimes. But lately, even she has stopped visiting me. I haven't seen her for a long time!"

"We hardly find any time, Deep Di. But you can once in a while!"

"You're right, Saket!" Deep Di muttered in a distraught voice. "How would you have time now? I've heard you've become a very big man. You own big cars and a big house. And you keep company with big people. I've also learnt that you've acquired all the 'merits' of big people. I've heard that you've started drinking too… Do you remember there was a time when you used to wear khadi clothes and talked a lot about serving the country? Ultimately, your true self has emerged in this manner!" Deep Di's face reddened. She started breathing fast. "It isn't your fault. Saket. It seems everyone has gone off the head!"

"…"

"I had thought if I died, you would at least cover me with a shroud… But you haven't left such a chance for me…"

Tears filled Deep Di's eyes. Resting her head on the spinning wheel, she closed her eyes.

Saket sat silent for a while. Then he got up. He walked down the stairs and as he was about to cross the road, he ran into Major Verma's daughter. That Camel-like girl had grown taller.

"I've got married, Sir!"

"I see! That's very good..."

"Do visit my house sometime, Sir. B-22."

"I shall certainly come." Saket wanted to get away from her but she stopped in front of him. "Sir, do you still have that bullock cart at the back of your house by which Devdas…"

She had hardly finished her sentence by the time Saket disappeared in the crowd.

Chhaya's eyes were gradually improving. She had even started reading and writing. But one day she was run over by a truck and died …

It was a year since Chhoti Amma passed away…

Roop had been married off. Her husband was a professor at a college in Kanpur. He was very rich. He possessed a car. She was living happily. She had called Anni to live in her house. He was studying there.

Nina was alone in that huge house. The house was desolated. At times she was troubled too much by her loneliness.

Dada Babu was no longer able to work as a watchman. He lived in Saket's house. He did some odd jobs whenever he could. In the meantime, Saket had engaged a new servant who looked after all the work inside and outside the house.

Nina appeared not concerned about the time when Saket came and went. She had given up urging altogether. Now she didn't say anything to anyone.

For Saket, the house was like a sarai. Most of the time he was on tour Nina had removed the photograph of Saket's deceased father from the wall and kept it among her Gods. She alone had been worshipping Amma's Gods now. She bathed them exactly like Amma did and made offerings of food just like her.

Nina tried to read but could not concentrate. She would read just a few lines and then throw the book down. She did some embroidery and she had kept fish of variegated colours in three or four small glass jars. She had painted large pictures of boatmen and hung them on the walls. Outside near die gate she had grown a large number of palm trees. In her bedroom, there was always a pile of coconuts.

One full moon night — she spent the whole night sitting on the terrace. She felt she was seeing the expanse of the sea all around her and the giant tidal waves were rising to the sky....

She stood up before daybreak, thinking it was time for the boatmen to return!...

Whenever Saket returned home, he experienced a fish-like smell, rather stench all around.

"Nina!" he called her occasionally and on such occasions she came up to him and started laughing hysterically. Her laughter scared him out of his wits. At home, Nina often wore a Nicobari dress, surrounded by pictures of boatmen with their nets and cars. Boats, only boats! And nothing but coconuts...!

"Don't you feel afraid being alone in such a big house?" Nina stood speechless when Saket asked her such a question.

Nina had become a victim of insomnia. She wasn't able to sleep even for a brief while... If the doctor gave her the injection to induce sleep, she started shrieking aloud.

"What has happened to you, Nina?" Saket came near her bed and stroked her head affectionately. And Nina burst into tears like a small girl, hiding her face on his lap...

The more medical treatment Saket arranged for her. the more her health deteriorated. Ultimately the doctor came to the conclusion that she had got tuberculosis...

Deep Di visited her occasionally and made inquiries about her health. Saket too was very anxious seeing her health steadily deteriorating. Finally, he decided it would be better to send her to the Bhuvali Sanitorium.

One day, thc car crossed the Yamuna bridge and after passing Shahadra, disappeared as it went speeding along the long and dusty roads!

NINETEEN

The climate of Bhuvali suited Nina very well. There were no coconut and palm trees, but she was excited by the pine and deodar trees which were equally tall. The air passing through the pine trees breathed fresh life into her. Gradually, Nina's health started showing some improvement...

Saket wrote letters to her and she wrote back..."The winds are very chilly here. The mountains are covered with snow. Very big, high mountains! How would people be living among these mountains...!" She wrote.

Twice or thrice, Saket himself came to look her up. She kept on talking about all sorts of things for hours. She said that she didn't feel at home being all alone. There was no human soul known to her. She insisted on getting back to Delhi.

Saket reassured her that she would soon be well and he would take her back to Delhi.

"You've really left me, isn't it? You've brought me to this place where 1 can't see anything beyond and where there's none whom I can call my own," she said with the obduracy of a child.

"How far would the seashore be from here?" she asked after a pause. "I can see no coconut trees around here..! On the full moon night, I tell you, I really get frantic. I see only waves rising and dashing around me. Devata had said that I would one day drown in the sea and die...I don't know how long I've been pining for the sea...!"

Saket kept his palm over her withered lips.

Nina's health improved still further after returning to Delhi. Saket took her to Shimla during the summer. She felt still better at Shimla. She looked healthy like before. But within two or three months of coming back to Delhi, there was a sudden change. She looked pale and anaemic again and as depressed and melancholy as before. The nurse said she was pregnant…

Saket returned from tour. He found her very tired…

"Will you accompany me to the market?" he asked.

"No!"

"Do you have a desire to eat anything in particular?"

"No!"

She had no strength left to go anywhere. She closed her eyes. She remembered the times when she used to sit alone in a boat and go far, far away!... One day, the sea was rough. The boat had capsized, and then, struggling against the waves, she had somehow reached the shore…!

Her eyes were fixed on a tree where at one time she had hung an earthen pot tied in a red cloth…!

Nina had grown blue flowers in pots. What an enthralling sight it had been to see the same flowers blooming in the jungle! The palm trees she had grown near the gate were now tall enough to reach up to her head. The pile of coconuts in her room had also become very big.

Deep Di came to her once in a way and gave medicines to her. She also brought fried fish from her house for Nina…

"Lately, I've been having some bad dreams. I think I'm not going to live long…"

Deep Di stroked her hand, "Why do you think like that? Illness can come to anybody…"

Tears welled up in Nina's eyes…

Saket had hung in his room a very big painting which resembled a woman. Whenever Nina went to that room, her eyes remained fixed on it…

Almost every night, her throat was dry. She groaned and cried painfully for water. But Saket sleeping next to her lay highly inebriated. Dada Babu came from downstairs and gave her water.

The doctor said all that was natural a result of an overdose of medicines... When Saket tried to give her medicine, she held his hand and urged him: "For God's sake send me to Nicobar… In this place. I am unable to live and unable to die…"

"Don't say such things!" Saket stroked her forehead, which was hot like a heated griddle. "Who is there in that place with whom you can stay…?"

Nina swallowed the bitter dose of medicine and muttered to herself: "Yes, I had my mother but she is dead. Now there isn't anybody…! I haven't got anybody anywhere…! But yes, there are at least the coconut trees! And the dusty seashore…! And lush green desolate islands. One needs only a little space to die in, whereas over there, vast lands are lying empty."

Tears streaked from her eyes. She searched for something in the ceiling. But she couldn't fix her gaze anywhere — it seemed to be suspended in a void, which was without any support …

The nurse said: "In her present condition, she would hardly survive."

Saket wanted to admit her to a hospital but she didn't agree. She started crying.

Roop had come from Kanpur after a long time. Since Anni was having holidays, he too had insisted on accompanying her.

"Bhabhi, come with me. We shall arrange for your treatment there…"

Nina shook her head.

All those expensive new sarees that Saket had brought at one time lay unused. Nina didn't wear them even once. She offered those sarees to Roop when she was going back.

Roop declined: "God has given me plenty of things…!"

"What am I going to do with these?" Nina said. "I know you have got plenty of things. There's nothing that you lack. Still, you take these sarees. Even if you don't wear them, just keep them with you. Under that pretext, you'll remember me at times."

Then she said after a brief pause: "I get very strange dreams these days, Roop! The walls of the house, and doors, arouse a feeling of disgust in me. I can't sleep. What has happened to me?"

Roop held her Bhabhi's hand and started crying.

When Saket returned after his tour of Assam, NEFA and Manipur, he found Dada Babu waiting at the gate. He was crying.

Saket was dumbfounded.

"What has happened, Dada Babu? What has happened?" he asked in panic.

Dada Babu informed him: "The mistress of the house has been missing for the past seven days. When I went to give her tea, I found her bed empty. I was in a real panic when I didn't see her till the afternoon. I informed the police. And I sent an urgent telegram to you. There was no news about her. I even sent a man to that lady teacher's house. But her house was locked."

Saket went inside. There was no trace of her anywhere.

All things in the house were in the same state as ever. Some of Nina's dirty clothes hung on the pegs. Some opened and half-opened medicine bottles. And on the walls hung the pictures of fishermen. A large number of multi-coloured fish were swimming in the glass jars. In the flower pot, were blue wildflowers.

Saket sat down with his hand on his forehead.

Several months passed without any information. Saket sent a series of letters and telegrams to Nicobar but got no satisfactory reply.

Some people said Nina must have committed suicide. Some thought she must have gone away to Andaman-Nicobar.

Saket just couldn't believe that in her state, she could have gone so far. Travelling that far involved countless problems. Sanctions from the concerned officials had to be obtained. Nina was capable of arranging all that, but how could she have done it in her state of health?

With such thoughts in mind, he asked Dada Babu one day to pack his luggage.

With just a few items of daily use and a few clothes packed in an attache, he went towards the Palam airport. While leaving, he told Dada Babu that he would be back in about ten day's time.

TWENTY

Saket got no information even after he went to Nicobar.

There was a big farm where the fishermen used to live. The dense forest had been cleared. A new colony of refugees had come up there. The road built by Saket had now become old. Ebony trees had been planted on both sides of those roads. A very big government hospital was also coming up. The Navy had taken possession of an island for its use. A giant ship of the Indian Navy could also be seen floating there.

Saket stood on the jetty to go to a nearby island. He was waiting for his steamboat. It was said that very few Nicobaris still inhabited that island. There were also some colonies of fishermen.

As he was about to board the steamboat, the old jawabdar ran into him. Bowing repeatedly, he greeted him respectfully. He said: "After you went away, the engineer gave us a lot of trouble. Even today all the labourers remember you. They seek God's blessing for you."

Saket, defeated and tired as he was, made the aged jawabdar sit by his side. When he made inquiries about Nina, the jawabdar gave him an astounded look.

"Some months ago. I did see her here once," The jawabdar said, passing his hand through his long grey hair. "She came to our jatt ha for getting work. But she was so ill and weak that nobody could have given her work. Even if she were given some work, she wouldn't have been able to do it. She had started collecting coconuts and dry betelnuts. She used to live near fishermen's huts. They say she had even given birth to a child. A few days later, she was found dead."

Saket went around the place where she had been living. Some coconuts and dry areca nuts lay scattered there even now. A rag from a saree still hung from a branch of a tree.

The Nicobaris showed him the place where she had been buried. Saket still couldn't believe it. Was she really dead?

He dug that place and found some bones scattered under the green grass.

The evening sun was sinking in the sea. The bottomless, boundless water suddenly acquired a touch of colour. Sailboats were returning towards the shore. But Saket saw nothing around him. With his eyes closed, he was lost in some thoughts.

A tribal woman had brought up the child. Saket took the child from her and brought him along.

He used to have his tent there at one time. Nina had grown all kinds of flowers there. Here both of them had stood getting soaked in the rain: She had been offended and had fled without a word. On this very rock, she had been standing like a mad person when he had to stay back since the motorboat had not arrived.

One whole age passed before his eyes and he shut his eyes tight.

The following day he returned home with his child.

Saket had completely changed. He had grown a beard. He also dressed himself shabbily, which gave him the appearance of a madman. He went to his work in that state for a few days. But he could not sit there and immediately returned home. He sat on the balcony, staring at the deserted roads.

An ayah had been engaged to look after the baby. Dada Babu ran around the house the whole day, carrying the baby in his arms.

Saket found the whole house terrifying. Such big rooms! High ceilings! If he coughed, the sound echoed as it would under a dome.

The palm trees that Nina had grown had dried up and looked like burnt stumps. The fish in the closed glass jars had died long ago. The pictures of fishermen on the wall had been devoured by white ants. The pots of blue flowers lay in disarray.

"What has gone wrong with you, I say?" Deep Di occasionally came and asked stroking his hair which was entangled like algae.

Saket continued to sit with a grim and glum face.

"Will you come to my place? You never eat properly," Deep Di said. "How can you go on like this? Whatever has happened, must be forgotten. Why don't you understand?"

Saket gave him an irritated look. Then he suddenly got furious: "Dada Babu, tell her to go away!"

Deep Di remained standing there, trembling like a flame. She couldn't understand what Saket had been saying…

Saket was scared of darkness. At times during the night, he felt as though he had heard Chhoti Ma's voice, at times the sound of utensils being flung and breaking on the floor.

He opened his eyes wide and peered through the darkness — indeed, someone had closed the adjoining room from inside and was shaking it violently...

He sat up on the bed and switched on the light. Nobody was there.

He tried to go back to sleep. He felt as though Chhaya was seated in front of him. her small fingers groping for something. And her small hands! He switched on the light and spent the whole night sitting on the bed.

Sometimes, during a brief spell of sleep he heard Nina's echoing laughter, and then some strange uproar and then some frightening sight…! People running with the tricolours in their hands. People advancing like a surging ocean. The sky reverberating with the cries of Inqilab Zindabad. Above the crowd, he saw a hazy picture —handcuffs on hands and heavy shackles on feet! An overgrown beard looking like hay. People gathered near the gallows. People groaning in a dark solitary cell, writhing in pain and dying…

Saket felt that someone was writhing and groaning in the next room—the same room as what he had seen in the Andaman Jail…!

In spite of the light, he felt his room was dark. He shrieked aloud.

Dada Babu rushed up, rubbing his eyes, he saw that Saket's whole body was soaked in sweat and he had fallen from his bed and lay unconscious.

TWENTY-ONE

His office colleagues came. Friends came. Several acquaintances and well-wishers came. Doctors were consulted. But Saket heeded none of them.

Tall grass had grown in the courtyard. He spent the entire full moon night on the terrace. Like Nina, he too saw surging waves all around. And just water everywhere!

Sometimes he went out all by himself. When he returned after a long time, he had the impression that Nina was standing on the balcony...!

He sat on the chair and spread his legs in front of him. Resting his forehead on his palm, he kept on brooding over something. He had a feeling that Nina had probably removed his shoes by that time!

He opened his eyes and realized that he hadn't put on his shoes at all that day. He had gone out of the house without wearing his shoes at all....!

Rattan visited him during the holidays. He asked: "Do you recognize me?"

Saket didn't reply.

Rattan's mother said affectionately: "Arrey, you've forgotten even your Tai, is it? When your mother died..."

Saket got up and walked away. He didn't allow anyone to come near him.

He sat day and night, wrapped in a blanket.

The cold wind was blowing. There was mist in the air. The entire sky was dark with black, dusty clouds. Saket walked in silence, wrapping a blanket around himself.

Passing many roads and lanes he stopped in front of a house. He knocked at the door.

"Who is it? Arrey, you...!"

Without a word, Saket entered the house and sat down.

"Where were you going in this cold?"

Saket made no reply.

Deep Di went in and made tea. She offered one cup to Saket. He kept staring at the cup.

"Drink, I say!"

He continued to stare.

"What are you staring at? Drink!"

Bowing his head, Saket started drinking tea.

"What has happened to you? You're in such a high position and you enjoy such a good reputation! My heart shudders to see you in these rags"

It seemed Saket hadn't reacted at all.

"You must be hungry. Will you eat something?"

Deep Di brought some salty snacks on a plate. Like a domesticated animal, he started eating, with his eyes lowered.

"You are not feeling comfortable here. Will you go out with me somewhere?"

He stared at Deep Di.

"What can I do for you? You live here. I shall take up a job again. I'll find some other work, but 1 won't let you live in any discomfort. My craving, of many births, would be fulfilled if I could be of some help to you…! But you're so hostile…!" Deep Di's voice choked.

Some grains of fried daal were sticking on Saket's lips. Deep Di wiped his lips with the end of her saree.

"You used to be so naughty at one time! You wiped your mouth with my washed saree! Do you remember?"

Those two individuals, as though seated in separate rolling boats, stared at each other.

"The time is up, Deep Di...!"

"Don't say that…!" Deep Di shrieked.

Sometimes the ayah brought the baby to Deep Di's house during the day. Deep Di bathed him and put him to sleep after giving him milk and gazed steadily at the sleeping baby…

The child was as naughty as he had been. The same nose! The same big eyes! The same ears! Exactly like him!

Deep Di had made dresses for the baby from the yarn she had spun herself. The baby chirped excitedly even from a distance ... and leaned forward to snatch her spectacles…

"Engineer Babu!" Dada Babu moved close to Saket very hesitantly one day. "How long will it go on like this?" Dada Babu's aged voice choked. "Go for your work, Engineer Babu!"

Saket sat cross-legged, covering himself with a blanket. He looked at the picture Nina had drawn at one time.

He closed his eyes — the fisherman's villages, thorny bamboo bushes, a spring close to the bushes, near the spring the bones pressed under the green grass, scattered coconuts — everything seemed like a dream to him.

"Dada Babu. I'm not at peace here," he muttered very slowly and groaned with unbearable pain.

When Dada Babu brought tea for him, he looked at him like a child: "Do you hear some loud noises during the night, Dada Babu?"

Dada Babu shook his head in astonishment. "No! There's no such thing — It's all an illusion."

"The world itself is an illusion, Dada Babu!..."

Dada Babu came rushing.

"Engineer Babu is missing! He hasn't come home since last night!"

Deep Di was startled: "Did he say anything before going?"

"No! I don't know anything at all…!"

"Since when is he missing?"

"Since yesterday."

"Why didn't you inform me earlier?

The baby in Dada Babu's lap was crying.

"Have you looked around properly?"

"I searched everywhere but didn't find Engineer Babu. Verma Babu said he had seen him at the railway station getting into the Howrah Mail. He had covered himself with a blanket…"

"Which Verma Babu?"

"From the military.... old Verma Babu....!"

Deep Di placed her finger on her lips — Howrah Mail, that's Calcutta.... that's the Andamans....!

Deep Di's colour paled.

"If he went to the Andamans, he won't ever return...!" she cried. Dada Babu was in terrible panic. The baby was crying at the top of his voice.

"Can you go with me, Dada Babu?" she shook Dada Babu's hand in excitement.

"Where?" Dada Babu's toothless mouth was agape.

"Calcutta. We can catch him if he hasn't boarded the steamer already. They say the steamer leaves once a week or so…!"

Deep Di was on the point of tears.

"Then do you think we'll be able to find our Engineer Babu ?" Dada Babu repeated in disbelief.

Deep Di was seated like a mad creature. Leaning out of the window, she kept staring at something. The baby was asleep in her lap. His throat was paining after crying the whole day. Dada Babu's body swayed with the jolts of the train... His toothless mouth was open. He was fast asleep…

Deep Di's hair was flying in the air. A taxi was speeding towards the Kidderpore Docks. She had just telephoned Howrah and learnt that a steamer was due to leave for the Andamans at nine-forty hours…

It was already nine thirty-five.

"Go fast. The steamer is due to leave…"

The driver accelerated the speed.

"Now only two minutes are left!"

The taxi went faster..... still faster…!

When Deep Di got off at the Kidderpore Docks she saw a steamer, looking like a demon — The anchor was about to be lifted — The steamer, with a shaky movement, began gliding away.

Thousands of hands waved in the air.

On the deck of the steamer stood a figure leaning on the railing, still like a statue and wrapped in a blanket. He had turned his face on the other side of the bank. Only his dark back was visible. Holding his blanket tight with both his hands, he was staring at the sky.

A great tidal wave rose and with its thrusts, dragged the swaying steamer away from the dock.

Deep Di wanted to leap towards the steamer, but couldn't do it.... she wanted to shriek, but couldn't do it... Her blue lips were caught between her teeth., and her eyes were wide open...

She pressed the crying baby hard between her arms and then resting her head on the little back of the child, burst into bitter tears like an innocent girl!

www.ingramcontent.com/pod-product-compliance
Ingram Content Group UK Ltd.
Pitfield, Milton Keynes, MK11 3LW, UK
UKHW042019190726
13854UKWH00005B/2361

9 789356 825963